TEMPTED BY THE TEXAN

KATHIE DENOSKY

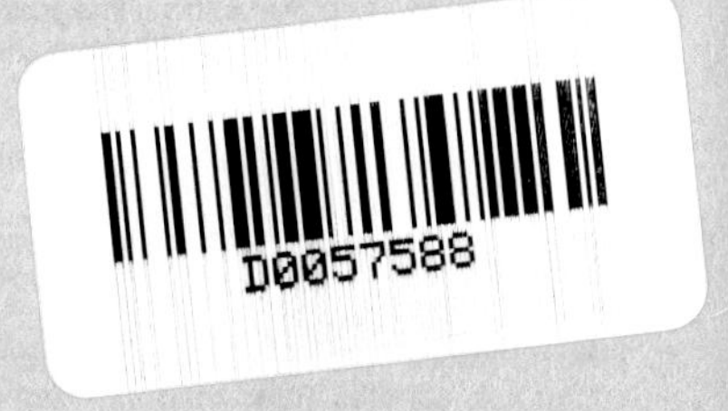

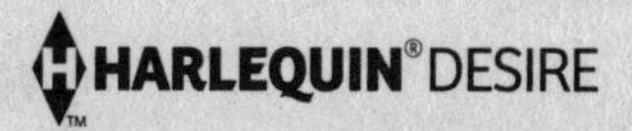

Recycling programs for this product may not exist in your area.

ISBN-13: 978-0-373-73442-9

Tempted by the Texan

This edition published by arrangement with Harlequin Books S.A.

For questions and comments about the quality of this book, please contact us at CustomerService@Harlequin.com.

Printed in U.S.A.

"You can't have it both ways, Jaron. You are either interested or you aren't."

"You're my sister-in-law's kid sister," he said stubbornly. "I'm just watching out for you."

"Oh, good grief! Get over it, Jaron." Mariah rested her hands on her sexy hips. "In case you haven't noticed lately, I'm no longer a naive eighteen-year-old girl. I've grown up. I'm twenty-five and perfectly capable of taking care of myself."

Jaron took a deep breath. Oh, he'd noticed that Mariah wasn't the teenager he had met when his foster brother, Sam Rafferty, married Bria Stanton. Back then Mariah had a crush on him, and although he had found her attractive, he knew that a nine-year age difference made him too old for her. But over the years, he would have had to be as blind as a bat not to notice that she had grown into a beautiful, sexy woman.

And that was the problem.

Interested didn't even begin to cover how he felt for Mariah.

* * *

Tempted by the Texan
is part of
The Good, the Bad and the Texan series—
Running with these billionaires will be one wild ride

Dear Reader,

When I first came up with the idea for *The Good, The Bad and The Texan* series, five of the six foster brothers' personalities were clear in my mind, and I knew exactly how I wanted their stories to unfold. But one brother was darker, more mysterious and reluctant to reveal much about himself. I found him extremely interesting, and as he made appearances in the first five books, I became even more intrigued by his smoldering sensuality and the attraction between him and Mariah Stanton, the sister of the heroine from book one.

In the sixth and final installment of this series, we finally discover the reasons behind rodeo cowboy Jaron Lambert's insistence that he's too old to become involved with Mariah. So please sit back and enjoy the ride as we find out what happens when a man with both physical and emotional scars finds his redemption in the arms of a woman who refuses to give up on him.

I'm going to miss the men from the Last Chance Ranch and hope you've enjoyed reading about how these bad boys became real good men. Sometimes rocky, sometimes filled with twists and turns, the road to love is never easy. But it's always worth the journey.

All the best,

Kathie DeNosky

CONTENTS

Kathie DeNosky lives in her native southern Illinois on the land her family settled in 1839. She writes highly sensual stories with a generous amount of humor. Her books have appeared on the *USA TODAY* bestseller list and received numerous awards, including two National Readers' Choice Awards. Kathie enjoys going to rodeos, traveling to research settings for her books and listening to country music. Readers may contact her by emailing kathie@kathiedenosky.com. They can also visit her website, kathiedenosky.com, or find her on Facebook.

Books by Kathie DeNosky

Harlequin Desire

The Good, the Bad and the Texan

His Marriage to Remember
A Baby Between Friends
Your Ranch...Or Mine?
The Cowboy's Way
Pregnant with the Rancher's Baby
Tempted by the Texan

Visit the Author Profile page at Harlequin.com, or kathiedenosky.com, for more titles!

TEMPTED BY THE TEXAN

Kathie DeNosky

This book is dedicated to my family,
Bryan and Nicole DeNosky, David DeNosky,
and Heath and Angie Blumenstock.
You fill my heart with love. It's a joy and
my privilege to be your mother.

One

After working all day on the ranch he'd bought a few months back, Jaron Lambert sauntered into the Broken Spoke looking for three things—a steak dinner; a cold beer; and a warm, willing woman for a night of no-strings-attached fun. But as he sat down at one of the tables and surveyed the dimly lit roadhouse, he knew he would be settling on the steak and beer, then heading back to his place—alone.

It wasn't that there weren't any women in the bar or that they hadn't paid attention to him when he entered. There were a couple playing pool and a few more sitting at two tables shoved together, looking as if they might be having a girls' night out. One of them had even smiled at him with a come-hither expression on her pretty face. But none of them piqued his interest enough for more than a passing glance. Maybe all the hard work to get his ranch in shape was catching up with him. More than likely it was because none of the women were a certain leggy brunette with the greenest eyes he'd ever seen.

Disgusted with himself for wanting a woman he knew damned good and well he could never have, he decided that he'd have been better off calling a couple of his five brothers to see if they wanted to join him for supper. If he had, at least he would have had someone to talk to while he ate. But they all had wives and kids now, and he could appreciate them wanting to spend the time with their families.

"What can I get for you, handsome?" a young, gum-snapping waitress asked, walking up to his table.

"I'll just have a bottle of Lone Star," he answered, deciding to forego the steak and just have a beer. As soon as he finished draining the bottle, he'd head back home to heat up a pizza and spend the rest of the evening in front of the television.

"One beer coming right up," she said, giving him a bright smile. After a minute, she returned, plunked down a napkin on the worn Formica tabletop and set the bottle on top of it. "You're Jaron Lambert, aren't you?" Her smile widened into a flirty grin when he nodded. "You won the World All-Around Championship at the National Finals Rodeo in Las Vegas just before Christmas, didn't you?"

"Yup." When she continued to stand there expectantly, he gave in and asked what he figured she was waiting on. "So you were there?"

"Oh, no," she said, shaking her head. "I couldn't afford a trip to Vegas on what I make here. I watched it on satellite TV." She gave him an enticing smile. "You sure looked sexy when they awarded you that buckle."

He could tell by the look on her face that she was interested in more than just talking about his big win in Las Vegas. Unfortunately for her, he wasn't. He had dodged more than his fair share of buckle bunnies—young women who flirted and hoped to sleep with a cowboy in possession of a championship belt buckle—over the years, and he was glad that part of his life was behind him. Hopefully with his retirement from rodeo after the finals a couple of months ago, that type of woman would lose interest in him and move on to another cowboy who didn't care if he became nothing more than a notch on a groupie's bedpost.

When he didn't respond to her comment and expectant expression, she shrugged one shoulder. "Well, if you need anything else—anything at all—just let me know."

"Thanks," Jaron said, taking a swig of his beer as he watched the waitress move over to another table where three men sat. It was clear one of them was going to get lucky and be invited to join her for a night of fun after she got off work.

After downing his beer, he got several dollars out of his wallet and tossed them on top of the table. There was no sense sitting there paying for more beer when he had a cold twelve-pack in his refrigerator at home.

But just as he started to get up, he noticed a woman walk through the door and up to the bar. He uttered a word under his breath that he reserved for smashed thumbs and card games with his brothers as he settled back down in his chair. What the hell was *she* doing here?

She was wearing a red dress that fit her body like a glove, and there was very little left to the imagination about the size of her breasts or the curve of her slender hips. He swallowed back another curse as his gaze drifted lower. That little red number she wore ended about midthigh and gave him more than a fair idea of how long and shapely her legs were. But it was the shiny black high heels she had on that caused him to grind his teeth. Those four-inch spikes were the kind a man looked at and knew the woman wearing them was just asking for him to take her home and pleasure her throughout the night.

Apparently, he wasn't the only guy in the room to notice. As Jaron watched, a seedy-looking cowboy with a Skoal ring on the hip pocket of his jeans and a leering grin walked up beside her. She glanced at the man, shook her head and turned back to speak to the bartender. It was crystal clear she wasn't buying what the good old boy was selling.

Jaron decided he wasn't going anywhere. At least not while Mariah Stanton was standing there looking for all the world like every man's midnight fantasy.

But as he watched the cowboy try to get her to pay attention to him, Jaron could tell from the look on the man's face that there was going to be trouble. The guy wanted her, and she didn't want any part of him. Unfortunately, the son of a bitch was either too drunk, too stupid or too determined to take no for an answer.

When the jerk reached out and took hold of her upper arm, Mariah recoiled, and that was when Jaron came up out of his chair to cross the room like a bull out of the bucking chute. Without a moment's hesitation, he planted his right fist along the man's jaw and watched the bastard hit the floor in an undignified heap.

"Jaron?" Mariah sounded startled when she looked over her shoulder at him. "What are you doing?"

"Saving your pretty little ass from getting into more trouble than you can handle," he retorted angrily.

"You knocked out Roy Lee!" one of the man's friends shouted, taking a step toward Jaron.

"Do we have a problem?" Jaron growled through clenched teeth as he quickly moved Mariah behind him out of harm's way.

A good six inches shorter than Jaron's six-foot-two-inch height, the man stared at him a moment then hastily shook his head. "I ain't got no quarrel with you, dude," he said, hastily taking a couple of steps in the opposite direction.

"Then, I strongly suggest you pick Roy Lee up off the floor and leave me and the lady alone," Jaron ordered.

As Roy Lee's friends hauled him to his feet, Jaron turned and, putting his arm around Mariah's waist, ushered her out of the place. She tried to pull away from him, but he tightened his arm around her and didn't stop as he guided her out the exit and toward her car in the parking lot.

"Jaron, have you lost your mind?" she asked as he hurried her along.

"What the hell do you think you were doing walking

into a cowboy bar looking for all the world as if you're advertising for a roll in the hay, Mariah?" he demanded when they reached her compact sedan.

"I don't look like I'm advertising for any such thing," she said, jerking away from him. "And what's wrong with the way I'm dressed? I think I look just fine."

Jaron folded his arms across his chest and let his gaze slide from the top of her dark brown hair to the soles of her impossibly high heels. That was the problem. She did look fine. Too fine.

He ignored her question and asked one of his own. "What in the name of Sam Hill did you think you were doing stopping by the Broken Spoke alone?"

"Not that it's any of your concern, but I had a dinner meeting in Fort Worth and on my way back home my car started making an odd noise. I managed to get it into this parking lot just before it died completely, and after I discovered that my cell phone needed recharging, I went inside to call a tow truck."

He watched her emerald eyes narrow as she glared at him. "And even if I had been there for other reasons, it's none of your business. I can handle situations like what happened in there all by myself."

"Oh, yeah? Is that why old Roy Lee put his filthy hands on you?" Jaron asked, doing his best to hold on to his temper. "The minute that bastard grabbed hold of your arm he made it my business."

When he'd seen the man touch her, Jaron had damned near come unglued. Aside from the fact that he took exception to any man forcing his attention on a woman when it was clear she didn't want it, the woman in question had been Mariah. As long as he had a single breath left in his body, nobody was going to treat her with anything but complete respect.

"Really? It's your business? You've made it perfectly clear all these years that you have absolutely no interest in anything I do." She shook her head. "You can't have it both ways, Jaron. Either you are interested or you aren't."

"You're my sister-in-law's kid sister," he said stubbornly. "I'm just watching out for you."

"Oh, good grief! Get over it, Jaron." She rested her hands on her sexy hips. "In case you haven't noticed lately, I'm no longer a naive eighteen-year-old girl. I've grown up. I'm twenty-five and perfectly capable of taking care of myself."

Jaron took a deep breath. Oh, he'd noticed several years ago that Mariah wasn't the teenager he had met when his foster brother Sam Rafferty had married Bria Stanton. Back then Mariah had had a crush on him, and although he had found her attractive, he knew that a nine-year age difference made him too old for her. But over the years, he would have had to be as blind as a bat not to notice that she had grown into a beautiful, sexy woman. And that was the problem.

Interested didn't even begin to cover what he felt for Mariah. He wouldn't call it love. Hell, he'd have to believe in the emotion before he could say that was what it was. But he did find himself thinking about her a lot, and whenever the family got together for birthdays dinners or holidays, he couldn't seem to take his eyes off her.

"I don't care how old you are. There's no sense in putting yourself into a dangerous situation," he insisted.

"Dangerous?" She laughed and the sound sent a shock wave of heat straight through him. She pointed toward the entrance to the bar. "Sam brings Bria here for dinner all the time. For that matter, the rest of your brothers bring their wives here, as well. We both know they wouldn't dream of doing that if they thought they were placing the women in jeopardy."

It was Jaron's turn to laugh. "Do you honestly think that some dust-covered cowboy would have the guts to try putting the moves on one of my sisters-in-law with my brothers right there to knock them flat?"

Continuing to glare at him, she shook her head. "I'm not going to get into a debate with you about your antiquated idea that women need a man's protection whenever they go out." She started to brush past him to go back into the bar. "I've had a trying day, I'm tired and I need to make that phone call."

"Not in there you're not," Jaron said, placing his hands on her slender shoulders to stop her.

"Jaron Lambert, I swear if you don't—"

Before he could stop himself, he pulled her close and brought his mouth down on hers to silence her. But the moment he tasted her perfect coral lips, he lost every ounce of sense he'd ever possessed and gave in to years of temptation and denial.

Wrapping his arms around her, Jaron settled Mariah against him, and the feel of her breasts crushed to his chest, her body touching his from their shoulders to their knees, set a fire in his belly that he thought just might burn him to a crisp. Without a thought to the consequences, he traced the seam of her mouth with his tongue to coax her to open for him. When she did, he slipped inside to explore her inner recesses.

As he stroked and teased her, she grabbed the front of his jeans jacket with both hands for support as she sagged against him. That fueled the fire in his belly to a fever pitch, and his erection was not only inevitable—it caused him to feel light-headed from its intensity. Tightening his arms around her, he held her to him and he knew the second she felt the evidence of his need when she shivered and pressed herself even closer.

His heart stalled as another wave of heat flowed through his veins. He had wanted her for so damned long, if he didn't put some distance between them, and real quick, he wasn't sure he would be able to. But when he tried to ease away from the kiss, Mariah's lips clung to his and he knew it was going to take every ounce of strength he could muster to move away from her.

Forcing himself to take a step back before she made him forget he was a gentleman, he took a deep breath. "What seems to be wrong with your car?"

"I…uh, I'm not sure," she said, sounding as winded as he felt. "I heard a noise and a few minutes later I noticed the lights were dimming. By the time I parked it here, they went out completely and the engine died. When I turned the key to restart it, all it did was make a clicking sound."

"It sounds as if you might have a bad battery or the alternator went out," he said, thankful to focus on something besides the enticing woman standing next to him.

It appeared that neither wanted to mention the kiss, and that was just fine with him. The less said about his lapse of judgment, the better.

"Is that expensive?" she asked, nibbling on her lower lip. She wasn't trying to be provocative, but it was all he could do to keep from kissing her again.

"Don't worry about it," he said, shaking his head. "I'll have my men come and get your car in the morning and see what they can do. I've got a hired hand who can fix just about anything with four tires and a motor."

"That's great, but how am I supposed to get home tonight?" she asked, rubbing her temple with her fingertips as if she might be developing a headache. A sudden rumble of thunder followed by a flash of lightning in the distance caused her to groan. "Great! Just great. I still have ninety miles to drive before I get home, my car won't run and now it's going to start raining. Could this day get any better?"

"It's been a rough one?" he asked, noticing the defeated expression on her pretty face.

She looked at him as though he might be one of the simplest souls she'd ever met. "Let me put it to you this way—I've definitely had a lot better."

As he stood there staring at her, he waged an internal battle with himself. It was getting late and there weren't a lot of choices. He was worn-out from working all day and she sounded as though she was exhausted from whatever had ruined hers. He could drive her down to Shady Grove, but he really wasn't looking forward to making the hour-and-a-half drive back as tired as he was—not when he had a very comfortable, fully furnished six-bedroom ranch house ten miles away.

"Don't worry about how you're going to get home," he said, glancing at his watch. "You can stay at my place tonight and drive back to Shady Grove in the morning after my men get your car fixed."

"I don't want to impose." A sudden gust of wind had her impatiently brushing her long dark brown hair away from her face as she shivered from the February cold. "Could you drive me over to Sam and Bria's?"

It would be the best for all concerned if he could take her to her sister and his brother's ranch. Unfortunately, that option wasn't on the table. "Sam and Bria left this morning to go down to Houston for a stock show."

She looked uncertain for several seconds and he could tell she was trying to think of something—anything—else she could do. When her shoulders sagged in defeat, he knew she'd reached the same conclusion he had.

She sighed heavily. "It doesn't look as though I have a choice, does it?"

He shook his head. "I've got five spare bedrooms and you can take your pick."

"All right," she finally agreed, opening her car door. She retrieved a short black leather jacket from the passenger seat and pulled it on, then used her remote to lock the car.

Neither spoke as they walked the short distance to his truck and he helped her into the passenger side of the cab. What could they say? He had let his guard down and given in to the temptation of kissing her. But it couldn't happen again. Now that she was going to have to spend the night at his place because her car had broken down, another kiss like the one he'd given her a few minutes ago could very easily push him over the edge and cause him to lose what little sense he had left.

When Jaron walked around the front of the truck to slide into the driver's seat, he stared straight ahead as he started the powerful engine. He still wanted her and he could only hope that he'd cool off on the ten-mile drive to the Wild Maverick Ranch, at least enough to get some sleep.

But as he steered the truck out of the parking lot and headed toward his ranch, he knew as surely as the sun would rise in the east tomorrow morning that wasn't going to happen. Now that he had tasted her sweet lips and held her soft body against his, he wanted a whole lot more. And that was something he knew for certain he could never have.

Mariah deserved a man who could offer her a future free of the emotional and physical scars of the past. Unfortunately, he had both.

When Jaron drove his truck beneath the arched entrance sign of the Wild Maverick Ranch, Mariah's heart skipped a beat. She still couldn't believe that he'd kissed her, let alone that she was going to spend the night at his new ranch.

When she was eighteen, she'd had a crush on him and dreamed of nothing more than having him feel as enamored with her as she was with him. He'd known about the infatuation, and instead of teasing her about it as some men might have done, he had been a perfect gentleman. He hadn't encouraged her in order to stroke his ego, nor had he discouraged her. He had simply ignored it and treated her the same as the rest of his brothers. She'd known he thought he was too old for her back then, and he'd been right. She hadn't been mature enough to handle a relationship with a man in his late twenties.

As the years went by and they saw each other at the family gatherings her sister held for the six foster brothers, she'd seen Jaron watch her and known he found her attractive. But to her disappointment, he hadn't asked her out or treated her any different than he had when she was a teenager.

Then as the brothers married and started their families, her relationship with Jaron had turned into a rivalry of sorts. Whenever one of the sisters-in-law became pregnant, Jaron insisted the baby would be a boy, while she just knew it would be a girl. But even as they argued about it, there had been an undertone of tension that had recently become so thick it was impossible to deny.

Mariah glanced at Jaron. But tonight something had changed between them. She'd known it the moment he punched the cowboy at the Broken Spoke. Although any of his brothers would have taken exception to the man grabbing her by the arm, Jaron had been absolutely furious. And if his reaction hadn't given her a hint that things were different between them, the kiss he had given her certainly had.

She had been kissed many times before, and although they'd been pleasant, none of them had been like the kiss Jaron had given her. There had been so much passion in the caress that it had been overwhelming. And what she couldn't get over was the fact that they had both ignored it, as if it hadn't even happened. They had started talking about her car problems and where she was going to stay for the night instead of addressing the fact that after all these years he had finally acted on their mutual attraction.

"Unbelievable."

"What's unbelievable?" he asked as he parked his truck in the four-car garage and pushed the remote on the visor to lower the door.

Unaware that she'd spoken her thoughts aloud, Mariah shrugged. "I was just thinking about my day," she lied.

"Some days are like that," he said, getting out of the truck. "Maybe tomorrow will be better."

"It has to be. I doubt it could get any worse," she said, opening the passenger door. Before she could figure out how to get out of the truck without breaking one of her high heels, or for that matter one of her ankles, Jaron was there to lift her down from the seat. His large hands wrapped around her waist caused her to feel warm all over. "Th-thank you."

"Would you like something to eat?" he asked as they walked through the door to the mudroom. "I've got a couple of frozen pizzas I can toss in the oven."

"No, thank you." She shrugged. "I had dinner after my meeting." She didn't add that she hadn't been able to eat due to the fact that during the meeting she had learned she was out of a job—effective immediately. "If you don't mind, I think I'd like to go on to bed."

"Of course not." He led the way down the hall to the stairs. "Bria and the other sisters-in-law made up all the rooms when they decorated the place, so you can have your pick."

"They did a fantastic job," she said, noticing the original paintings by a popular Western artist hanging on the wall as they climbed the steps. The decor reflected the Wild Maverick's new owner and his cowboy lifestyle.

"They did a better job than I would have done, that's for sure," he commented. When they reached the top floor, he opened the first door they came to and flipped on the light switch to turn on the bedside lamps. "If you don't like this room, there are four more to choose from."

"This will be fine," she said, looking around. Decorated in a cool shade of green and cream, the colors complemented the Native American artwork on the walls and the handwoven area rugs on the hardwood floor. "Bria and the others should consider going into interior decorating."

"I was going to leave the bedrooms empty, but Bria pointed out that I needed to furnish them in case I had guests." He shrugged. "I doubt that I'll ever have that many, since all of my brothers live close by."

"If you don't think you'll need the rooms, why did you buy such a big house?" she asked, unable to see the logic in him paying for something he didn't intend to use.

"I wanted the land," he admitted. "It's close enough to all of my brothers' ranches that we can help each other out when needed and not have to drive more than an hour or so to get there." He gave her a half smile. "The house just came with it."

She wasn't surprised Jaron wanted to live close to his foster brothers. From what her sister had told her, all six of them had been in trouble with the law when they were teenagers and the foster-care system had given up on them as lost causes. They'd been sent to the Last Chance Ranch, and thanks to a special man named Hank Calvert and his unique way of using ranch work and rodeo to teach them life lessons, all of the boys had worked through their troubles and turned their lives around. They had all become honest, productive adults, and because of their similar problems when they were boys and having no families to return to once they were of age, they had bonded into a very close family of their own.

"I wish I could live closer to Bria and Sam," Mariah said wistfully. Living a couple of hours away, she didn't get to see her only sibling nearly as much as she would have liked.

Jaron surprised her, and if his expression was any indication, he might have stunned himself when he stepped closer and brushed a wayward strand of her hair from her cheek. "Maybe one day that real estate place you work for will open a branch office somewhere around here and you'll be able to live closer to your sister."

She knew he meant the gesture as comforting, but

his gentle touch and the knowledge that she no longer had a job with the company caused her to blink back tears. "I doubt…that will ever happen."

"What's wrong, Mariah?" His deep baritone was filled with gentle concern.

"Nothing," she lied. "It's been a really tough day. And one that I would just as soon forget."

She didn't want to go into the dismal turn her life had taken. She'd lost a boyfriend, a roommate and her job in less than twenty-four hours, and when she'd left Fort Worth after her meeting, she'd planned on having a good cry once she got home. The boyfriend hadn't really bothered her because they hadn't been seeing each other more than a couple of weeks and their relationship hadn't been serious. In fact, it never would have been. They both knew that one day they'd stop seeing each other and she hadn't even bothered mentioning that she was seeing him to her sister. But the loss of her roommate and her job had been devastating. Her roommate had left without notice, and she was going to have to find a way to pay both halves of the rent. Without her job, she had no way of doing that. But since her car broke down and she couldn't be alone for that cleansing cry, she'd just have to keep her tears at bay for a while longer.

Jaron seemed to hesitate a moment before he wrapped his arms around her and drew her to his broad chest for a supportive hug. "I'm sure you'll feel better after a good night's sleep."

"I doubt it, but thanks for the encouragement." She knew he was only trying to set her mind at ease, but the feel of his strong arms around her was absolutely wonderful, and without thinking she snuggled closer into his reassuring embrace.

She felt him go perfectly still. “Mariah…I think I’d better let you get some sleep.”

She nodded but couldn’t bring herself to pull away from him. “That would probably be for the best,” she agreed.

When neither of them moved, Jaron used his index finger to lift her chin until their gazes met. “Tell me to get the hell away from you and leave you alone, Mariah.”

Staring up at him, she knew she should do as he commanded. But without hesitation, she slowly shook her head. “I can’t do that, Jaron.”

“What I’m feeling right now is wrong,” he warned, his expression testament to his inner turmoil. “I’m no good for you.”

“That’s your opinion,” she said softly. “It isn’t mine and never has been.”

He stared at her a moment before he shook his head. “Don’t say that, Mariah.”

“I’m just being honest, Jaron,” she answered quietly.

He closed his eyes a moment, as if struggling with himself, before opening them to capture her gaze with his. Slowly lowering his head, he kissed her so tenderly it sent shivers of anticipation up her spine. But instead of him releasing her and taking a step back as she thought he would do, his mouth settled more fully over hers for a deeper caress.

When his tongue touched hers, the heat that she’d

felt the first time he kissed her came rushing back and caused her knees to give way. As he caught her to him, he stroked and teased her with precise care and Mariah felt the growing evidence of his need against her lower belly. An answering desire caused an empty ache deep in the most feminine part of her. Her heart skipped a beat when she realized where things were going. She knew without question that if she asked him to call a halt to things, he would do it no matter how difficult it was for him. But that wasn't what she wanted. She had waited for what seemed like an eternity for him to hold her like this and now that he was, she never wanted it to end.

Feeling as if her head was spinning from the intense longing coursing through her, she was vaguely aware that he tightened his arms around her a moment before he lifted his head to stare down at her. "Mariah, kissing is one thing. But it's going to go way beyond that if we don't stop this right now."

"Jaron, I don't care how far this goes," she said honestly. She raised her arms to circle his neck and tangled her fingers in his thick dark brown hair brushing the collar of his shirt. "I've wanted you to hold me like this since the moment we met."

"Don't say that." When he closed his eyes, a muscle twitched along his lean jaw and she knew he was struggling to do what he thought was right. "I'm not the kind of man you need, Mariah."

"That's where you're wrong, cowboy," she whispered, cupping his cheek with her palm. "You're exactly what I've always needed."

Two

Jaron felt as if he'd been struck by a bolt of lightning when Mariah touched his face with her delicate hand. He might have had a chance to harden his resolve and not let things go too far between them if she hadn't admitted that she had always needed him. But her softly spoken words and the feel of her touch sent a flash fire streaking through his veins and made thinking clearly all but impossible. He'd wanted her for years, and not allowing himself to hold her, kiss her, had been his own personal hell.

He knew it was wrong—that he should walk away and leave her alone. But when he looked down at the woman in his arms, he knew in his heart that wasn't going to happen. He needed Mariah more than he needed his next breath, needed to lose himself in her softness and forget for one night that she could never be his.

When she pressed a kiss to the exposed skin at the open collar of his shirt, then looked up at him, the desire in her brilliant green eyes robbed him of breath. She for damned sure wasn't helping him win the battle over the hormones racing through his veins at the speed of light.

"Jaron, I know you need me just as much as I need you."

There was no sense in denying it. Hell, he was certain she could feel the evidence pressed against her. But he had to give her one last chance to save them both from doing something he knew as surely as he knew his own name they would both end up regretting with the morning light.

"Are you sure about this?" he asked. "Once that line is crossed, there's no going back, Mariah."

"I've never been more sure of anything in my entire life," she said without hesitation. "I don't like the way things have been between us recently, and I don't think you do, either."

"I'm not promising anything beyond tonight," he warned her.

She shook her head. "I'm not asking for more."

She might not be asking, but he knew Mariah well enough to know she wasn't a one-night stand kind of woman. If she slept with a man, she would expect it to be the start of a relationship. Unfortunately, he had wanted her for longer than he cared to remember and turning back now just wasn't an option.

Groaning, he buried his face in her silky dark brown

hair and tried to remind himself of all the reasons making love to Mariah would be a bad idea. For the life of him, he couldn't remember a single one. A man had his limits, and Jaron knew that he had reached the end of the line with his.

For the past several years he'd fought against giving in to the attraction between them. But now that he'd finally held her soft body to his and tasted her sweetness, he couldn't seem to stop himself. Maybe it was due to the years of denial or more likely the loneliness that had settled in when he watched his brothers with their families—knowing that due to the fear he had of turning out to be like his father he would never allow himself to have a family of his own. He wasn't entirely sure what the reason was, and it really didn't matter. He'd deal with the guilt and regret in the morning. Tonight he was going to forget about the problems making love to her would cause and love Mariah as if there was no tomorrow.

"Let's go to my room," he suggested, taking her hand in his to lead her down the hall.

As they entered the master suite, Jaron flipped the light switch to turn on the bedside lamps, casting a soft glow over the king-size bed. Closing the door behind them, he immediately took Mariah in his arms and lowered his head to rain kisses along her cheek, down the column of her neck to her collarbone.

"Are you protected, Mariah?" he asked, removing her black leather jacket, then kissing the satiny skin exposed by the dropped shoulder of her slinky red dress.

"I… Um, no," she said, sounding delightfully breathless.

"Don't worry." He continued to nip and taste her. "I'll take care of it."

When he raised his head, the desire clouding her pretty green eyes rendered him speechless. She was without a doubt the most beautiful, exciting woman he had ever known, and unless he missed his guess, she didn't have a clue how hot and sexy she was.

"There's probably…something you should…know," she said, sounding a little unsure.

"Have you changed your mind?" he asked, torn between knowing it would be in the best interest of both of them if she had and at the same time dreading her response.

"No, I haven't changed my mind." There wasn't a moment's hesitation in her answer and, God help him, he was thankful.

"Whatever it is, it can wait until later," he said, bending to remove his boots.

"But I think it's something you'll probably want to know," she said, sounding a little uncertain.

Straightening, he gave her a quick kiss. "Do you want to make love with me, Mariah?" When she nodded, he shook his head. "That's all I need to know."

He didn't want to hear confessions about other men she'd been with. All he wanted to do was focus on bringing her the most pleasure she had ever experienced in any man's arms.

As he kissed his way across her collarbone, she reached up to push her dress down her arms. Stopping her, he shook his head as he lightly skimmed his hands across her bare shoulders then down her arms, taking the stretchy fabric as he went. "I've been thinking about peeling this little number off you since I watched you walk into the Broken Spoke."

When he lowered the knit dress to her waist, then slid it over her shapely hips and down her long legs to lie in a pool around her shiny black high heels, his heart stuttered at the sight of her. Her strapless black lacy bra and matching panties barely covered her feminine secrets and sent his blood pressure up into stroke range. Put a pair of those fancy wings on her back and Mariah could easily model for that famous lingerie company every man with a pulse found so fascinating.

"You're gorgeous," he said, feeling as if all of the oxygen had been sucked from the room as he squatted down to remove her shoes.

"Thank you." When he straightened, she stepped forward to reach for the snaps on his chambray shirt. "But you're a little overdressed for this, don't you think, cowboy?"

As he watched, Mariah unfastened his shirt, pushed it from his shoulders and tossed it aside to place her hands on his bare chest. His pulse sped up and it felt as though he'd been branded where her soft palms rested. How many times had he speculated how her delicate hands would feel when she touched him like this? Nothing he could have imagined came close to the excitement racing through his veins at that moment.

"I knew your body would be beautiful," she said as she traced the valley between his pectoral muscles with her index finger.

"Looks can be deceiving," he said, thankful that she

couldn't see the ugly imperfections he'd spent most of his life trying to hide.

Before she could ask him what he meant, Jaron unbuckled his belt, released the snap at the top of his jeans, then gingerly eased the zipper down over his persistent erection. Shoving his jeans and boxer briefs to his ankles, he quickly stepped out of them and kicked them to the side.

He silently watched as Mariah's gaze traveled the length of his body. He could tell she was trying not to be conspicuous. But when she noticed his arousal, her eyes widened a moment before she lifted them to meet his.

"I'm just a man, darlin'," he said, reaching behind her to unfasten her bra. "You aren't afraid of me, are you?"

"N-no," she murmured. "Being afraid of you has never crossed my mind."

"Good." Tossing the scrap of black lace to the pile of clothes on the floor, he kissed her deeply before cupping her breasts in his palms as he stared into her pretty eyes. "I promise we'll be perfect together, Mariah."

"I—I know," she said, shivering when he kissed each one of the taut peaks, then moved his hands to slip his thumbs into the waistband of her panties.

He slowly lowered them over her slender hips and down her thighs, and when he tossed them aside he stepped back to appreciate her gorgeous body. Everything about her was perfect, and he felt humbled at the knowledge that a woman as stunning as Mariah would want to be with him.

"You're amazing," he said, his voice sounding a lot like a rusty hinge.

When he took her in his arms, the feel of her soft, feminine body pressed to his much harder one sent a shock wave the entire length of him. He had never allowed himself to speculate what it would be like to hold her nude body to his—to have their bare skin touching. But he knew for certain that he never could have imagined anything as erotic or sensual as what he was experiencing at that moment.

When she sagged against him, Jaron swung her up into his arms and carried her over to place her in the middle of his king-size bed. Her long dark brown hair spread across his pillow and her lithe body lying on the black satin sheets was an image he knew he would never forget.

Opening the bedside table's drawer, he removed a small foil packet and, tucking it under his pillow, stretched out beside her to take her in his arms. "Do you have any idea how beautiful you are?" he asked, not really expecting an answer.

"Not as beautiful as you are," she said, raising her arms to his shoulders. From the look on her face, he knew the moment she felt the scars on his shoulder that he normally kept covered. "Are these from participating in the rough stock events for so many years?"

He didn't want to lie to her, but he didn't want to explain, either. "Everyone who competes in rodeo has a few," he said, making sure he kept his answer vague. He did have a couple of scars from riding the rough stock, just not the ones under her fingertips.

To distract her from asking more about them, he fused his mouth with hers and kissed her with all of the need he had denied for almost as long as he had known her. Sweet and soft, when her lips melded with his, Jaron forgot about anything but the woman in his arms and the heat inside him that had built to a fever pitch. He had wanted Mariah for years and he found it damned near impossible to think about anything but burying himself so deep inside her that they lost sight of where he ended and she began.

Unable to wait any longer, he kissed his way down to her collarbone as he moved his hand along her side to her hip and beyond. Caressing her satin skin, he parted her to stroke the soft folds with tender care. The fire inside him threatened to burn out of control at her readiness for him. She needed him as much as he needed her.

"Mariah, I promise next time we'll go slower," he said, reaching for the packet under his pillow. "But right now, I need to be inside you."

"I need that…too," she said, her tone breathless.

He quickly arranged their protection and nudged her knees apart to rise over her. When she raised her arms to his shoulders and closed her eyes, he leaned down for a brief kiss.

"Open your eyes, Mariah," he commanded.

When she did, he captured her gaze with his as he guided himself to her. The desire and the depth of emotion he saw in her rapt expression were humbling, and unable to wait any longer, he slowly, gently moved forward.

The mind-blowing tightness as he carefully entered her robbed him of breath. It felt as if she had never…

He immediately froze. "Mariah…are you a virgin?"

he asked hesitantly. He hadn't even considered the possibility that she'd never been with a man. But he was for damned sure thinking about it now.

"Y-yes," she answered.

Jaron closed his eyes as he waged the biggest battle he'd ever fought in his entire life. The logical part of his brain advised him to get out of bed, send her back to the guest room, then go downstairs to his game room and drink himself into a useless stupor. But his body was urging him to complete the act of loving her—to make her his and damn the inevitable consequences.

She must have sensed the conflict within him because, wrapping her long legs around him, she captured his face with her soft hands. "Jaron, I want this. I want you."

He might have been able to win his inner struggle if he hadn't seen the desire coloring her smooth cheeks or heard the urgency in her sweet voice. But the combination of her heartfelt declaration and the feel of her tight body surrounding his was more than he could resist.

"Forgive me, darlin'," he said, pushing himself forward to breach the thin barrier blocking his way. Her eyes widened and a soft moan passed her parted lips when he sank himself completely inside her.

Holding his lower body perfectly still, Jaron kissed away the lone tear slowly trickling down her cheek. He hated that in order to love Mariah this first time he had to cause her pain. But as he felt her body relax around him, he knew that she was adjusting to his presence and, easing himself back and then forward, he set a pace he hoped would cause her the least amount of discomfort. He knew she probably wouldn't derive much pleasure from their lovemaking, but that wasn't going to keep him from trying to give her whatever pleasure he possibly could.

As the driving force of the tension holding them captive increased, Jaron held himself in check until he felt Mariah begin to respond to his gentle movement. Only then did he increase the depth and strength of his strokes.

When he felt her tiny feminine muscles begin to tighten around him, he knew she was close to realizing the satisfaction they both sought and, reaching between them, he touched her in a way he knew would send her over the edge. Her fulfillment triggered his own and, gathering her close, he wasn't sure he wouldn't pass out from the extraordinary sensations of his release.

Collapsing on top of her, Jaron buried his face in her silky hair and tried to catch his breath as he slowly drifted back to reality. He had never experienced anything as intense or as meaningful as being one with Mariah.

As his strength returned, he eased himself to her side and pulled her into his arms. "Are you all right?"

With her head pillowed on his shoulder, she nodded as she rested her hand on his chest. "I'm fine." She yawned. "That was amazing."

He could tell by the sound of her voice that she was drowsy and, remembering that she'd mentioned having a rough day, he kissed the top of her head and reached over to turn off the bedside lamp. "Get some rest, darlin'."

He'd barely finished making the suggestion before he could tell that Mariah had dozed off. Long after he was sure she was sound asleep, he continued to hold her close as he stared up at the ceiling. What the hell had he done?

No matter how much he would like to go back to the way things had been between them in the past, it would never be the same again. He'd not only crossed the line with her, he had taken something that she could give to only one man.

He closed his eyes as he fought the need building inside him once again. He wanted her, and just the thought that he had been the first man to touch her like this sent heat streaking throughout his body with lightning speed.

It hadn't even crossed his mind that she might still be a virgin. Hell, Mariah was twenty-five years old and he knew for certain that over the years she'd dated several men. So why him? Why had he been the one she chose to be the first man she made love with?

Unable to think clearly with Mariah in his arms, Jaron contented himself with simply holding her while she slept until sometime around dawn, when he reluctantly eased away from her and got out of bed to pick up their clothes. Folding hers, he placed them on the bench at the end of the bed, then took a quick shower and got dressed.

As he started to leave the room, he turned to gaze at the beautiful woman sleeping peacefully in his bed. How had he let things get so out of hand with her? Why had he ignored that voice of reason in his head, telling him to walk away before he did something he was sure to regret? And how was he going to be with her at family gatherings without losing his mind from wanting her and not allowing himself to touch her?

Guilt and regret so strong it threatened to choke him settled in his gut and, shaking his head, Jaron headed downstairs for a stiff drink. He needed to shore up his resolve and do what he knew was right and would be the best for Mariah. As soon as his men repaired her car, he was going to send her on her way and hope like hell one day he could forget the most incredible night of his entire life.

When Mariah awoke the following morning to sunlight peeping through a part in the drapes, two things were immediately apparent—she was in Jaron's bed and he wasn't with her. She was a little disappointed, but not really surprised. Bria had told her that ranchers usually started their days before dawn and sometimes worked until well past sundown. Now that Jaron owned the Wild Maverick Ranch, it stood to reason that he would keep those hours, as well.

Lying there surrounded by his clean masculine scent on the black satin sheets, Mariah's heart skipped a beat as she thought about the shift in the direction of their relationship. After all these years, Jaron had finally recognized she was no longer an eighteen-year-old girl with stars in her eyes. He had finally seen her as the woman she had become, albeit almost grudgingly. But she was certain that even he would have to admit that what they had shared was beautiful.

As she thought about his hesitancy, she frowned. Why had Jaron kissed her, made love to her, if he had been so reluctant? She might not be as experienced as a lot of women her age, but she knew beyond a shadow of doubt that it wasn't because he hadn't desired her. In fact, it had been as if needing her was the last thing he wanted. But he hadn't been able to stop himself.

Confused by his reaction, she got up and collected her clothes from the bench at the end of the bed, then she went into the master bathroom for a shower. They needed to talk, and his usual brooding silence wasn't going to cut it this time. She wanted answers and she wasn't going anywhere until she got them. What they had shared last night had been too meaningful to be dismissed. Nor was she going to allow him to ignore their lovemaking as if it never happened the way he'd ignored their first kiss.

Twenty minutes later as Mariah pulled on the clothes she'd worn the night before, she made the bed, then opted to carry her shoes instead of trying to navigate the circular staircase in four-inch heels. As much as she liked the boost the shoes added to her five-foot-five-inch height, she wasn't willing to take the chance of breaking her neck before she confronted Jaron and got the answers she wanted.

Picking up her jacket and purse, she left the master suite to go downstairs in search of Jaron. She was a bit surprised to find him seated at the table in the breakfast nook, drinking a cup of coffee. She had fully expected him to be somewhere outside with his ranch hands, doing whatever ranchers did.

"Good morning," she said, walking over to set her things on one of the chairs.

He gave her a silent, stoic nod as he got up to take a mug from the cabinet above the coffeemaker. "You like cream in your coffee, don't you?"

"I'm surprised you know that," she said, pulling a chair from the table to sit down.

"I've watched you drink coffee with dessert at our family dinners for years. You and Lane's wife, Taylor, are the only ones who don't drink it black." He shrugged one broad shoulder as he reached into the refrigerator to take out a dairy carton. "Will milk be okay? It's the closest thing I have to cream."

"That's fine." She'd known he watched her whenever they were together, but she hadn't taken into consideration that he might have actually paid attention to mundane things like how she took her coffee.

"Would you like something to eat?" he asked as he set the cup in front of her. "I can make you some toast, but that's about it. I haven't hired a housekeeper and I'm not much of a cook."

"No, thank you. I don't usually eat breakfast." She stared at him as he sat back down at the table. There was no easy way to bring up what he was trying to sidestep. And knowing him the way she did, there wasn't a doubt in her mind that he would try to avoid discussing the shift in their relationship if he could. "We need to talk about last night," she finally stated.

He eyed her warily for a moment before he asked, "Are you all right?"

"I'm fine," she said, frowning. "Why wouldn't I be?"

"Until last night, you had never made love." His dark blue gaze caught and held hers for several seconds before he added, "I know I hurt you. I'm sorry."

"That's it?" she asked incredulously. "You gave me the most incredible experience of my life and all you can say is you're sorry?"

"What do you want me to say, Mariah?" His even tone and calm demeanor infuriated her.

So angry she found it impossible to sit still, Mariah rose from the chair to pace the length of the kitchen. "How about admitting that our lovemaking meant as much to you as it did to me?" She stopped to glare at him. "And don't you dare give me the excuse of being too old for me, because we both know it would be a total lie."

A fleeting shadow in his dark blue eyes was the only indication that he wasn't as removed from the situation as he would like her to believe. "Last night shouldn't have happened," he said, his stubborn calm irritating her as little else could. "I took something from you that I had no right to take, Mariah."

"My virginity." When he nodded, she shook her head. "You didn't *take* anything," she stated flatly. "It was my call to make. I *chose* to give that to you."

"Last night was a mistake," he insisted.

"No, it wasn't. A mistake is taking it for granted that your roommate isn't going to move out without telling you and leave you owing the entire month's rent. Or believing that you have job security and then suddenly finding yourself out of work," she shot back. "And we won't even go into how big a mistake it is to believe that your car is reliable when it's ten years old and makes more odd noises than you can count." Mariah shook her head. "Last night was the only good thing that happened to me yesterday, and I'm not going to let you dismiss it as if it meant nothing."

Jaron frowned as he got up and walked over to stand in front of her. "You lost your job?"

"Yes, but that's not the issue here." She refused to allow him to divert the conversation. "We're not talking about my work situation. We're discussing what happened between *us*."

"There is no us, Mariah," he said quietly as he rested his hands on her shoulders. The heat from his palms felt absolutely wonderful, but she did her best to ignore it. "I told you I wasn't promising anything past last night," he continued. He shook his head. "That hasn't changed, darlin'."

Staring up at him, she could see the determination in his eyes and the stubborn set of his jaw. She would have about as much luck convincing elephants to roost in trees as she would getting him to admit that what they'd shared was special. It simply wasn't going to happen.

Resigned, she walked over to slip on her high heels and gather her jacket and purse. "I don't suppose your men had a chance to see about my car?"

He dug into the front pocket of his jeans and, producing the keys to her car, handed them to her. "All you needed was a new battery."

When he placed the keys in her hand, his fingers brushed her palm and a streak of electricity zinged straight up her arm. She could tell by the slight tightening of his jaw that he felt it, as well.

"I'll pay you for the repair as soon as I get a new job," she said, walking toward the door.

"Don't worry about it," he said, following her. "It didn't cost that much."

"I most certainly will pay you back for the battery. I may be out of a job right now, but I do have my pride," Mariah said, turning back to glare at him. "I'm not a charity case."

"I never thought you were," he said, looking a little bewildered. "I'm just trying to help you out."

"I don't need your help," she said pointedly. "The only thing I need from you is an explanation of what changed between us and why you're wanting to go back to the way things were. But you refuse to talk to me about it."

She knew she was probably overreacting to the situation. But she was frustrated beyond reason and besides, if she didn't vent in some way, she couldn't be sure she wouldn't bop him on top of his stubborn head with her purse.

"Do you have any prospects of finding another job?" Jaron asked, following her out the door. "Do you need help making the rent since your roommate moved out? I could loan you—"

"Don't you dare offer me money," she warned, her anger rising to the boiling point. "After last night, you would be the last person I—"

"I'd like to do something to help," he interrupted, reaching up to run his hand through his dark brown hair as if he was trying to think of a way to help her out. He hesitated for a moment before he offered, "I still need a housekeeper who cooks. And the job comes with free room and board. You could work here until something better comes along." He didn't sound all that encouraging, and she knew it was nothing more than a token gesture. He didn't want her to take the job and had only offered it to her because he felt guilty.

"You're offering me a job and a place to live?" she asked incredulously. She didn't know whether to laugh out loud at his erroneous assumption that she could cook or be highly insulted that he thought she was so desperate she would accept his offer.

"The job is yours if you want it," he said, looking less than enthusiastic about having her around all the time. She had no doubt he expected her to turn it down and that was exactly what she intended to do.

"No, thank you," Mariah answered as she carefully descended the steps. If her mother hadn't taught her to be a lady, she'd gladly tell him what he could do with that job.

As she navigated her way across the yard to the driveway, hoping that she could keep from breaking an ankle or at the very least one of the expensive four-inch heels, she thought about the opportunity Jaron had inadvertently handed her. It would be poetic justice if she did accept the job. By living under the same roof with him, he certainly wouldn't be able to avoid her, nor would she let him forget the special night they had shared. And as for making his meals, it would serve him right if he had to eat her cooking.

But the more she thought about it, the more sense it made. She needed a job, and he owed her an explanation that she was determined to eventually get from him. What better way to do that than by seeing him every day?

The only drawback she could see about taking the job was the possibility of losing what was left of her sanity from dealing with a man who made a habit of closing himself off. And then there was the problem of her sister accusing her of being impulsive again when Bria learned Mariah was living at the ranch with Jaron. But if she could find out the reason behind his insistence that he was no good for her, it would be worth it.

When she got into her car, she glanced up at the house to see Jaron still standing on the porch, watching her. His arms were folded across his broad chest and he was leaning one shoulder against a support post. He looked so darned good to her it took her breath away.

Mariah worried her lower lip as she weighed her options. If she drove away, she might never get the answers she wanted from Jaron. And if she stayed, she might get an explanation that she didn't want to hear. Unfortunately, she would never know unless she took the chance.

Taking a deep breath, she reached for the door handle. She might be setting herself up for a huge fall, but she just couldn't pass up the opportunity to settle things with Jaron Lambert once and for all.

Jaron frowned when he watched Mariah open the car door. What was she doing? She had rejected his guilt-induced job offer outright, and he had been greatly relieved. Why wasn't she leaving and getting on with her life, so he could try to get on with his? He had made it perfectly clear there was nothing to talk over and that they'd never be more than good friends.

Or could she be having more car trouble? That had to be it, he decided. Her car was older and had so many miles on it that he'd been surprised it had only taken a battery to get it going that morning.

By the time she made her way back to the porch in those ridiculously high heels, he was reaching for the cell phone to call Billy Ray to come up from the barn to see about her car again. But when she climbed the steps to stand in front of him, the defiant look on her pretty face stopped him cold.

"I changed my mind. I'm taking the job you offered me until I can find an office management position. I expect you to be in Shady Grove first thing Saturday morning with your truck to help me move," she stated flatly. Turning, she added as she descended the steps to go back to her car, "And don't be late. I want to get settled in before I have to start the job on Monday morning."

Shocked all the way down to his size-twelve Tony Lamas, all Jaron could do was stand there staring as he watched her march back down the steps and out to her car. As she drove away, he couldn't help but wonder what the hell had just happened. He'd only offered her the job of housekeeper and cook as a token gesture because he'd been sure she would turn it down. And she had. So why had she changed her mind?

Rubbing at the sudden tension building at the back of his neck, Jaron watched her car disappear down the lane leading to the main road before he turned and walked back into the house. What was he going to do now? He couldn't rescind the job offer. He'd brought it up and Mariah had accepted it. As far as he was concerned, that was as good as a written contract.

But what was he going to do about living in the same house with her? How was he going to keep from going completely insane from the temptation she posed day in and day out? And why was there a part of him that wasn't the least bit sorry that she had taken the job?

Three

Late Saturday afternoon, Jaron carried the last of Mariah's things into the Wild Maverick ranch house and wondered how one woman could possibly need so much stuff. She had two huge boxes alone that had been marked "shoes." Why did she need so many? All he had were his dress boots, a couple of pairs of work boots and a pair of athletic shoes he wore when he worked out.

For reasons he didn't want to delve into, he had decided to move her into the room he'd shown her the night he brought her home with him from the Broken Spoke, instead of the housekeeper's quarters off the kitchen. And it was just as well that he had. The closet down there was way too small and would have never held all of her clothes and shoes.

"Is that the last of the boxes from my car?" Mariah

asked, sticking her head out of the walk-in closet when he entered the bedroom.

He nodded. "That's the last of it."

"Just be glad I donated a lot of clothes and household items to the crisis center," she said, laughing as she walked out of the closet to get one of the containers of shoes. "If I hadn't, you'd probably be carrying in boxes until well after midnight."

"Do you want this in the closet?" he asked, stepping forward to pick up the big box for her.

"I could have carried that myself," she said, following him.

Setting it in front of the built-in shoe racks, he shook his head. "My foster father would come back and haunt me if I let you do that. If he told us once, he told us a hundred times that a man should never let a woman carry anything unless both of his arms were broken."

"The Cowboy Code?" she asked, smiling.

Jaron nodded. "Hank Calvert had his own set of rules to live by and they're damned good ones."

"Bria told me that Sam and the rest of your brothers feel the same way," Mariah commented as she opened the box and surveyed the contents.

"We wouldn't be the men we are today if not for Hank," he admitted. "Among other things, he taught us what it meant to have integrity and be respectful of others."

She nodded as she picked out a couple of pairs of high heels. "I never got to meet Hank. When Bria started having family dinners, I was away at college, and by the time I graduated, he had passed away."

"He was one of the best men I've ever had the privilege to know," Jaron said, meaning every word of it. "He made everyone around him want to be a better person."

"From everything I've heard about him, he must have been a wonderful man," she agreed, bending over to pluck more shoes out of the box.

As he stood there staring at her pairing up shoes, he completely forgot what they had been talking about. Swallowing hard, Jaron did his best to concentrate on anything but the woman next to him. The light scent of her herbal shampoo, the sound of her soft voice and the enticing sight of her shapely bottom when she bent over to take more shoes from the box were sending him into sensory overload and playing hell with his intention to forget the most incredible night of his life.

When the region south of his belt buckle began to tighten, he decided a hasty departure would be in both of their best interests and, carrying the last box into the closet for her, he turned toward the hall. "I'll let you get the rest of your things put away. If you need me for anything, I'll be downstairs."

Before she had the chance to tempt him further, Jaron went down to his office, walked around the desk and plopped down in his desk chair. What the hell had he gotten himself into?

He couldn't be in the same room with Mariah for more than five minutes without burning to hold her, kiss her and a whole lot more. But he refused to allow that to happen again, even if he did end up in a constant state of arousal for as long as she resided at the ranch.

As he sat there shoring up his resolve, his gaze

landed on the only thing he had kept from his life before being sent to the Last Chance Ranch—the reason he couldn't allow himself to get involved with Mariah. Encased in a small acrylic cube, the creased and tattered Dallas bus pass represented his escape and freedom from years of physical abuse at the hands of a man who never should have been allowed to procreate.

Reminded of his dismal childhood, Jaron took a deep breath. He had been afraid that no one would believe a thirteen-year-old kid when he'd told them that his old man had killed his mother. But he had skipped school that day anyway and used his lunch money to buy a bus pass to police headquarters downtown. At first, he'd been right—no one had taken his claims seriously. Even the rookie patrolman assigned to take his statement had treated him like a child with nothing more than a grudge against his father.

But when Jaron had shown the officer the scars on his back and told the man that Simon Collier had threatened to kill him and dispose of his body the way he had done with his mother, they'd immediately started paying more attention to what he had to say. A caseworker from Family and Protective Services had immediately been called, a photographer had taken pictures to document the ugly evidence of the abuse marring his skin and a warrant for aggravated battery of a child had been issued for his father's arrest.

Jaron had been upset that they were focused on apprehending his father on charges of child abuse rather than the murder of his mother. But he needn't have worried. True to form, old Simon had allowed his temper to get away from him when he'd seen that Jaron had been the one who'd turned him in to the law. During his tirade, he'd shouted that he should have done away with him at the same time he killed Jaron's mother. Unfortunately, during the ensuing investigation and trial, DNA evidence had linked his father to at least four more homicides of women with the probability that there were several more. But DNA analysis hadn't been as developed back then and what evidence they'd collected for some of the other murders had either been destroyed or contaminated.

But his dad had been convicted for the murder of Jaron's mother, and the only other good that had come out of the trial was the judge had allowed Jaron to legally have his last name changed to his mother's maiden name.

Unfortunately, that hadn't been enough to erase his connection to the bastard who spawned him. Every foster family he had been placed with had looked at him as if he'd killed those women himself, and it hadn't been long before he'd got in trouble with the system for running away. But when he'd been sent to the Last Chance Ranch he'd had no reason to run. He'd been accepted for himself, and not rejected for what his father had done.

Hearing Mariah start down the stairs, Jaron clenched his teeth and vowed not to bring that kind of ugliness into anyone's life, and especially not hers. He'd never intentionally been cruel to anyone, but how could he be certain that he hadn't inherited something from his father that would rear its menacing head at some point in the future? He couldn't. And unfortunately, he didn't see any way that would ever change.

"Do you have anything else in your freezer besides frozen pizza?" Mariah asked, laughing as she reached for another slice. She was still frustrated with him, but her anger had cooled enough that she could see the humor in his choice of convenience food.

When she'd finished arranging her shoes on the built-in racks in the closet, she'd come downstairs to ask if he wanted her to make them sandwiches for dinner. But Jaron had suggested that she put together a salad while he popped a pizza in the oven for their dinner. She'd offered to bake it, but he'd pointed out that her job as cook and housekeeper didn't start for another couple of days and until then she was his guest.

"Pizza and burritos are about the extent of what's in the freezer," he said, shrugging. "The first thing you'll have to do is go shopping for whatever you need."

"I'm good at shopping," she said, smiling. She failed to add that her kind of shopping didn't include produce or anything else that couldn't be zapped in the microwave or didn't have directions on the side of a box.

"I've already added you to the approved users on the credit card I've designated for household expenses," he said, taking a drink of his beer. "Buy whatever you need for the house."

"Do I have a household budget to go by?" she asked. "I don't want to overspend."

Her statement drew a rare chuckle from him. "Spend as much as you want." He named an amount that was more than she'd earned in a year working at the real estate management company. "If you need to go over that, let me know and I'll have the card limit increased."

"Unless it's for a state dinner at the White House, I can't imagine anyone needing that much for groceries," she said incredulously. She'd known Jaron was wealthy, the same as his brothers were, but she'd had no idea. "Is there anything specific that you would like for me to buy?"

"I like pizza," he said as he picked up another slice.

"What man doesn't?" she asked, smiling.

"Hey, it's easy and doesn't require a lot of cooking skills," he said, giving her a smile that sent heat streaking all the way through her. "I also really liked that apple pie you made a few years back for my birthday. One of those once in a while would be nice."

"I'm surprised you remembered that," she said, wishing that he hadn't. There was no way under the sun that she could make another one without Bria standing beside her telling her step by step what to do.

"It was really good," he said, nodding. "That was the closest I've ever had to something that tasted as good as Bria's apple pie."

"I'll put that on the list," she said, deciding to call Bria as soon as she and Sam got back from the stock show tomorrow evening. She not only needed her sister's help making an apple pie, she needed the title of a really good, really easy-to-follow cookbook and help with a comprehensive grocery list of things to stock the pantry and freezer. "What else do I need to get besides food?"

He looked thoughtful a moment. "Well, you might want to get whatever you'll need for cleaning the house. I've got a few things, but when I moved in Bria suggested that I wait until I hired a housekeeper so whoever it was could buy the products they preferred."

More comfortable talking about cleaning than she was cooking, Mariah nodded. "Is there anything else I need to pick up while I'm in town?"

"I don't think so." He finished his beer then got up from the table to put the can in the recycle bin under the sink. "Really whatever you see that you think we need for the house or you want for cooking or cleaning is fine."

How was she supposed to know what she needed in the kitchen when she didn't know how to cook?

Deciding it was time for a change of subject, Mariah rose to clear the table. "Besides cooking, cleaning and shopping, is there anything else I'm supposed to do?"

He stared at her for a moment before he slowly shook his head. "Not that I can think of. Why?"

"I'm just trying to make sure I understand the job description," she said, rinsing their plates and loading them into the dishwasher.

"You didn't say, but what happened with your job?" he asked, his tone a little hesitant.

"Cutbacks," she answered as she wiped off the table. "The company decided to concentrate on the more lucrative rental properties in cities like Dallas and Houston than smaller towns like Shady Grove."

"Were you offered a job if you were willing to relocate?" he asked, frowning as he leaned back against the counter.

"They offered, but I turned it down." She shook her head. "I didn't want to move that far away from Bria, Sam and little Hank. They're the only family I have."

Walking over to stand beside her, he raised his hand as if he intended to touch her cheek, then quickly lowered it to his side. "That's not true, darlin'. You have the rest of us."

A shiver of excitement slid up her spine when she realized he was fighting the urge to touch her. But she did her best to ignore it. He was probably trying to make her feel better and nothing more. "Thanks."

"It was pretty rough losing your parents in that car accident in your junior year in college, wasn't it?" he asked, his tone sympathetic.

Nodding, she had to clear her throat before she could answer. "It was pretty rough, but it would have been worse if I'd been younger."

"Yeah, I lost my mom when I was six," he said, surprising her. In all the years she had known him, she had never heard him mention his biological family before.

"What happened?" she asked.

"I'm not sure." He stared at her a moment, then shook his head. "It doesn't matter. One day she was gone and I knew I'd never see her again."

"I'm so sorry, Jaron," she said, placing her hand on his arm. "At least I got to have my parents with me until I was grown."

He shrugged. "I survived."

"What about your father?" she asked.

His jaw tightened a moment before his expression turned to blank indifference. "He…went away when I was thirteen and I haven't seen him since."

She could tell it bothered him more than he was letting on, but she wasn't at all surprised that he dismissed losing his parents as if it wasn't a big deal. If there was one thing she had learned over the course of the past several years it was that Jaron Lambert didn't talk about himself. Ever.

As they stood there staring at each other, she realized her hand still rested on his arm. But it was the spark that had ignited in his striking blue eyes that took her breath away.

"I…um, probably should get back to putting my things away," she said, thinking quickly as she started to pull away from him.

He placed his hand over hers to hold it in place as if he had found comfort in the gesture. "You've got all day tomorrow to get your things organized," he reminded. "I'm sure you're tired from packing the past few days and all the other things you had to do to get ready for your move to the ranch. Why don't you take the evening off and we'll catch a movie on one of the satellite channels?"

His suggestion surprised her, but what shocked her more was the tension surrounding them. The slight abrasion of his callused palm on her skin and his heated gaze holding her captive was more sensual than she could have ever imagined. But she did her best not to show she was affected by it in any way. If she did, it would give him the perfect excuse to shut her out the way he'd done the morning after they'd made love.

"I think you might be right about taking a break." She laughed to cover her reaction to him. "There was so much to do the past few days, I am pretty tired. I just hope I can stay awake long enough to watch the entire show."

He suddenly dropped his hand and took a step back as if he realized he was still touching her. "In other words the movie needs to be fast paced?"

"Yes, but I'm not a big fan of movies that will scare the stuffing out of me," she admitted.

"I'll keep that in mind," he said, standing back for her to precede him down the hall to the media room.

Once she and Jaron were seated on opposite ends of the big brown leather couch, he turned on the biggest television she'd ever seen and they settled back to watch five unlikely characters defend the galaxy from an evil warlord. Resting her head against the buttery-soft leather, Mariah thought about the bizarre turn her life had taken. Never in a million years would she have dreamed that what seemed to be the worst day of her life had worked out to be the best or that it would lead to her living with Jaron on his ranch.

Yawning, she felt her eyes growing heavy and did her best to focus on the television screen. The next thing she knew, Jaron was touching her arm.

"Mariah, it's time to go upstairs to bed," he said gently.

Blinking, she sat up. "But I'm watching the movie."

The sound of his deep laughter enveloped her like a

comfortable quilt and sent a warm feeling all through her. "Darlin', the movie is over."

She glanced at the TV to see the movie credits scrolling up the screen. "I must have been more tired than I thought."

He nodded. "You fell asleep about fifteen minutes into the story."

"Why didn't you wake me?" she asked, rising to her feet.

"You were sleeping so peacefully, I figured you needed the rest." He switched off the television and got up from the couch. "It's no big deal. If you want to know how it ends we can watch the movie another time."

"I'd like that. What I saw was entertaining," she said, covering a yawn with her hand.

"I think it's time we turn in for the night," he said, placing his hand on the small of her back to guide her toward the door. "You're exhausted and I have to be up early to ride the fence in the south pasture."

"You don't have your men do that?" she asked as they climbed the stairs.

"In winter, they have Sundays off after they get the morning chores finished," he answered, stopping at the door to her room. "I'm going to check out what needs to be done and let them know so they can make the needed repairs before they move a herd of steers to that pasture in a couple of weeks."

From what Bria had told her, any rancher worth his salt knew everything that was going on around his ranch and worked in conjunction with his hired hands to get things done and keep the operation running smoothly.

"It sounds as though we'll both be busy tomorrow. After I finish organizing my things, I plan on taking an inventory of the pantry and starting my shopping list."

He looked thoughtful for a moment. "Since we both have a lot to do and I'm not in the mood for pizza two nights in a row, why don't we plan on going out for supper tomorrow evening?"

"I'll take you up on that offer," she said, smiling. The more time they spent together in a relaxed setting, the better the chance of him letting down his guard and opening up to her.

As they stared at each other, her breath caught at the longing she detected in his steady gaze, and when he lifted his hand like he was going to cup her cheek, she thought he was going to kiss her. But as if he realized what he was about to do, he let his hand drop to his side and took a step back.

"Good night, Mariah. Sleep well." His low, intimate tone sent a shiver of desire straight up her spine.

"Good night, Jaron."

After entering her room, she closed the door and released the breath she had been holding. Just when she thought he was going to give in to the magnetic pull drawing them together, he'd stopped himself.

Mariah sighed heavily as she got a nightshirt from the dresser and headed into the bathroom to change. She had always been told that patience was a virtue. But whoever came up with that old saying had never dealt with Jaron Lambert. He was without a doubt the most frustrating, controlled individual she had ever met.

But that was about to change. She had seen a slip

in his ironclad restraint the other night when he hadn't been able to resist making love to her. And if it happened once, it could happen again.

With renewed determination, she stared into the mirror at the woman staring back at her. "It's past time Mr. Lambert's self-contained little world is shaken up. And you're just the woman to do it."

As he followed Mariah and the hostess through the restaurant to a table at the back of the room the following evening, Jaron looked around and hoped they didn't run into one of his brothers and their wives. That was unlikely, since he'd chosen a roadhouse outside Waco instead of having supper at the Broken Spoke in Beaver Dam. But meeting up with his family would open a whole can of worms that he'd just as soon keep sealed for a while longer.

His brothers had been after him for the past few years to ask Mariah out, and he would just as soon avoid having to explain that they weren't dating but she was living with him at the Wild Maverick. The situation was complicated and he wasn't entirely sure he understood his reasons for offering her a job himself. As for trying to explain it to his brothers, the interrogation that was sure to follow would make a military tribunal look like a walk in the park.

"I didn't realize they have a live band and dancing," Mariah said as he held the chair for her to sit down. Her delight was evident and he knew she was going to want to stick around for the dancing after they ate.

Taking his seat on the opposite side of the small

table, he shrugged. "What the house band lacks in talent, they make up for in enthusiasm."

"I can dance to just about anything," she said happily.

He barely managed to stifle a groan as the sweet sound of her voice wrapped around him. Mariah was without a doubt the most beautiful, exciting woman in the entire restaurant and she was letting him know that she wanted him to dance with her later. Unfortunately, she was with a man who hadn't been born with the dancing gene, like his foster brother Nate. To say that Jaron had two left feet would be an act of kindness. But as awkward as he felt on a dance floor, he wasn't about to let some other guy touch Mariah. If he had to, he'd pay the band a week's pay to play nothing but slow songs, then stand in one spot, hold her close and sway in time to the music the way his brother Ryder had always done.

He wasn't going to examine his decision too closely. If he did, he would have to admit that the thought of another man holding her close caused him to feel as though someone had punched him in the gut. It wasn't something he was the least bit comfortable with, nor was he happy about it.

"Did you find a lot of things that need to be repaired while you were out riding the pastures today?" she asked as they looked over the menu.

"More than I would have liked," he admitted, relieved to focus on something else. "The previous owner was older and lost interest in keeping things in good repair."

"The house seems to be in good shape," she said,

closing the menu and placing it on the table. "Did you have to make a lot of changes before you moved in?"

Jaron shook his head. "His daughter had the house remodeled before she put the ranch up for sale." When their server came to take their order, Jaron told him what they wanted, then waited for the man to walk away before he continued, "There are a few things I'd still like to change, but for the most part, I'm pretty happy with the house."

"The house is beautiful." She looked puzzled. "I can't imagine what you'd want to change about it."

"I'd like to take down the wall between the family room and media room," he answered, taking a sip of his water. "The house already has a formal living room, but it isn't big enough for the whole family to get together. I want a room big enough for us to gather and not be crowded."

Mariah nodded. "I love when your family has a party or dinner."

He frowned. "You're part of the family, too."

"Not really." She shrugged one slender shoulder. "I'm only included because I'm Bria's sister and have nowhere else to go for holidays."

Her statement surprised him, and without thinking, Jaron covered her hand with his where it rested on the pristine tablecloth. "You're just as much a part of the family as any of us, and I don't want to hear you say otherwise, Mariah."

"Th-thank you," she said, her eyes dewy with unshed tears. "That means a lot."

He hated seeing the sadness in her eyes, and at that

moment he knew he would do anything to make her happy, even if that meant making a fool of himself on the dance floor later. "Why don't we concentrate on finishing supper and then stick around for the dancing?"

"I'd like that, Jaron. Thank you."

Her sweet smile sent heat streaking through every vein in his body, and as he stared into her emerald eyes, he suddenly realized that he still held her delicate hand in his. For the life of him, he couldn't bring himself to let it go, nor did he seem to be able to look away.

What the hell was wrong with him? He didn't want to lead her on, nor did he want to fuel the need that burned in his gut every time he was close to her. Why couldn't he stop himself from touching her?

Thankfully, the server arrived with their food, breaking the tension building between them, and Jaron took a deep, fortifying breath. He was going to have to be extremely careful or else he was going to make the same error in judgment he'd made a few nights ago—something he couldn't allow himself to do. No matter how much he wanted to make love to Mariah, he had to stay strong and resist the temptation. He wasn't right for her and no amount of lovemaking would ever change that.

They both remained silent while they ate, and by the time they were finished with the meal, Jaron couldn't have said whether he'd had a rib-eye steak or a piece of worn boot leather. Through the entire meal all he'd been able to think about was holding her while they danced, and he knew as surely as he knew his own name he was in for a night of frustration, ending with a shower cold enough to freeze the tail feathers off a penguin.

When the band started warming up, he glanced over at Mariah, and the twinkle of excitement in her eyes was enough to convince him that he'd endure whatever hell came his way. There was no way he was going to disappoint her.

"I think I'll go freshen up before the dancing starts," she said, rising from her chair.

He waited until she disappeared down the hall leading to the ladies' lounge before he rose from the table, walked up to the bandstand and pulled five one-hundred-dollar bills from his jeans pocket. Handing it to the band's front man, he explained what he wanted, then with the man's assurance that the majority of the songs during the first set would be slow ones, Jaron walked back to the table and waited for Mariah to return.

"Are you ready to kick up your heels, cowboy?" she asked, smiling as she sat down on the chair beside him.

"I think I'd better warn you that I'm not much for dancing," he said, wondering if he'd ever seen her look more beautiful.

"I know," she said, grinning. "I've been attending family parties for years and I've never once seen you dance."

He shrugged. "That's because I'm not of a mind to make a fool of myself."

She cupped his cheek with her soft palm and sent his blood pressure up a good fifty points. "You're not going to make a fool of yourself, Jaron. If you'd like, we can dance the slow dances and if someone asks, I'll save the faster ones for him."

Her long, dark brown hair framed her pretty face and hung over her shoulders to cover her breasts. It made him want to run his fingers through the silky strands. But it was what she was wearing that sent his pulse into overdrive. Dressed in tight-fitting designer jeans with rhinestones on the hip pockets and a shimmery dark purple top, she had to be revving the engine of every guy in the place. The thought of another man holding her while they two-stepped around the dance floor caused him to grind his teeth. Even though he had no claim on her and had no right to make one without entering into a relationship with her, Jaron made a vow right then and there that he'd be damned before he watched her dance with anyone else.

"Like hell," he muttered as the band broke into the first notes of a popular slow country song.

"What was that?" she asked, leaning close.

Fortunately she hadn't heard him, and he didn't intend to enlighten her on his inner struggle. "I can't believe I'm going to say this, but let's dance, darlin'."

Rising to his feet, Jaron reached for her hand to lead her out onto the dance floor. As he took her into his arms, he surveyed the restaurant and caught several men watching Mariah. The appreciative looks on their faces did little to improve his dour mood.

But he quickly forgot about the other male patrons in the restaurant as he pulled Mariah a little closer. The feel of her lithe form rubbing against him as they swayed in time to the music caused him to react in a very predictable, very male way. All he could think about was the night he'd made love to her and how her soft body had felt as they moved together in perfect unison.

Telling himself to move away before he did something stupid, he made the mistake of glancing down at her delicate hand resting on his chest. Even through his chambray shirt, the warm feel of her palm sent a shock wave of need to the core of his being. Without another thought to the consequences, he lifted her chin with his forefinger and covered her mouth with his. Her sweet lips clung to his, fueling the rapidly building fire within him, and he couldn't have stopped himself from deepening the kiss if his life depended on it.

Forgetting where they were, he coaxed her to open for him and slowly, thoroughly savored her. He had a feeling he could quickly become addicted to Mariah's sweetness, and if that wasn't enough to scare him senseless, the fact that she could make him forget where they were and what they were doing was.

"This was a bad idea," he said, breaking the kiss and putting a little space between them.

"Why do you say that?" she asked as she looked up at him.

Jaron could tell by the awareness in her green gaze that she'd felt the evidence of his need and knew exactly what he'd meant by the comment. "Mariah, I'm not what you—"

"Save it, Jaron," she interrupted him. "I've heard it all before. You're too old for me. Or you're not right for me. Or whatever else you've come up with to use as an excuse to put distance between us." She pulled away from him. "I'm ready to leave."

As he followed her back to their table for her to collect her jacket, Jaron took a deep breath. He had been fooling himself to think he could be that close to her without wanting more. The magnetic pull between them was too strong for that to ever happen.

As he watched her walk briskly toward the restaurant's exit, he cursed his weakness and the need for her he couldn't seem to keep under control. He hadn't intended to piss her off, but it was probably just as well that he had. Maybe if she was mad at him, she'd be able to do what he couldn't seem to do himself. And that was to make him keep his hands off her.

By the time they reached the parking lot, Jaron practically had to trot to keep up with Mariah—a good indication of just how upset she was with him. Before he could reach her to help her into his truck, she climbed up into the passenger seat and slammed the door.

So much for dancing with her to make her happy, he thought as he got into the truck and started the engine. The ten-mile ride back to the Wild Maverick was an uncomfortably silent one, and by the time he parked the truck in the garage, he figured she would get out of the truck and go straight upstairs to her room.

But when they entered the kitchen she turned to face him. "Jaron, don't you think it's past time that you were honest with both of us?" she asked point-blank.

He wasn't going to insult her intelligence by asking her what she meant, but he wasn't going to talk about it, either. Instead of answering, he chose to remain silent.

After a few tense moments, Mariah shook her head. "We both know you have feelings for me. But you can't or won't allow yourself to admit that. I want to know why."

"I've told you before," he stated.

"Not good enough." She held up her hand to stop him from responding. "I don't want your standard excuses. I want the truth, Jaron. And until you can give me that, I'd just as soon you don't say anything at all." Without giving him a chance to respond, she turned and walked down the hall toward the stairs.

As he watched her go, Jaron knew she was right. She deserved his honesty. But as much as he would like to tell Mariah about himself, he'd much rather endure her anger than to have her look at him the way some of the foster families had—with a mixture of fear and suspicion.

Four

As Mariah tried to organize the things she had bought at the grocery store on the pantry shelves, she couldn't help but think about what had happened with Jaron at the restaurant the evening before. They'd had a nice dinner and he had suggested they stay afterward to dance, even though it was something he didn't like doing. He had even kissed her while they were dancing. Then, just when she thought he might be ready to admit that there was more going on between them than friendship, he'd stopped himself and reverted back to keeping her at arm's length.

Why did he have to be so darned stubborn? And why couldn't he at least give her an explanation for why he felt the way he did?

She had no idea what could be holding him back. But

telling her he was too old for her or that he wasn't right for her were excuses, not reasons. There was more to it than their age difference and she was determined to find out what it was and if he'd let her, help him move past it.

Deciding there was no easy way to get him to open up to her, she sighed and turned her attention back to the task at hand. She checked the list she had printed from the website of a popular cooking show. She had bought every spice they suggested, even if she didn't have a clue what she was supposed to do with them.

In hindsight, she probably should have called Bria for advice on what to get to stock the pantry and freezer. Her sister would know what all the spices were used for. But she had decided not to bother Bria. For one thing, she was busy chasing after a very active two-year-old and didn't have a lot of free time. And for another, Mariah was reluctant to tell Bria about accepting Jaron's offer to be the housekeeper and cook for the Wild Maverick Ranch.

Aside from the fact that her sister would have reminded her that she didn't know the first thing about cooking, Bria would have probably felt compelled to be the concerned big sister and warn her not to get in over her head or to count on things working out the way she wanted. But Mariah had accepted the job with her eyes wide-open and wasn't expecting anything more than getting the answers she wanted from Jaron.

"It looks as if you have enough food here to feed an army," Jaron commented from the doorway.

Startled by the unexpected interruption, Mariah jumped and placed her hand over her racing heart. After carrying in the groceries for her, he had gone outside to help his men with some repairs to one of the barns and she hadn't heard him reenter the house.

"Good heavens, Jaron! You scared me…out of a year's growth," she said, trying to catch her breath.

"I called your name when I stopped in the mudroom to take off my boots," he said, motioning over his shoulder with his thumb toward the kitchen.

"I must have been concentrating on getting all of these things put away and didn't hear you," she said, brushing past him to enter the kitchen. Glancing at the clock, she walked over to the sink to wash her hands. "After you brought in the groceries for me, I started putting everything away and lost track of time. I'll have your lunch ready in a few minutes. Will a sandwich and chips be okay?"

"That's fine," he said, nodding. "I'll help."

"Did you and your men get the repairs made in the barn?" she asked as she gathered the things she needed to make them ham-and-cheese sandwiches.

"Yes and no," he said, taking plates from the cabinet to set the table.

"How does that work?" she asked, laughing. "You either did or you didn't get things fixed."

His low chuckle sent a warm feeling throughout her body. "We got everything done on the list of things that needed repairing, then we found one of the stall doors has a broken hinge and another stall that needs a few boards replaced."

"It sounds as though keeping things in good shape

is a never-ending job," she said, setting a small platter of sandwiches on the table.

"Welcome to the world of ranching, darlin'," he said, holding her chair for her. When she sat down, he took a seat at the opposite end of the table. "Our foster father always told me and my brothers that if we couldn't find something that needed to be done, we weren't looking."

She laughed. "From everything I've heard about Hank Calvert he was a wonderful, very wise man."

"I don't know of any better," he agreed. "I don't even want to think about where my brothers and I would be if we hadn't been sent to the Last Chance Ranch. He saved us from ourselves and we wouldn't be where we are today without him."

They fell silent for several minutes as they ate before Jaron spoke again.

"I...want to talk to you about last night," he said, his voice hesitant.

Mariah stared at him a moment, wondering what he wanted to say. Had what she'd said to him the night before gotten through to him? Was he finally going to open up to her?

"All right." Her appetite suddenly deserting her, she placed her half-eaten sandwich on her plate. "What do you want to discuss, Jaron?"

"I want to apologize for kissing you." He shook his head. "It shouldn't have happened."

"Oh, good grief, Jaron!" She picked up her plate, got up from the table and carried it over to scrape the remainder of her lunch into the garbage disposal. Putting the plate into the dishwasher, she added, "If I hear you say that one more time, I think I'm going to be sorely tempted to throttle you." She turned to glare at him. "Get a clue, cowboy. Kissing me is something you obviously want to do or it wouldn't keep happening. And as for your apology, there is absolutely no reason for it. I wanted you to kiss me, and the night we made love, I wanted that, too. So keep your 'I didn't mean to do that' or 'it won't happen again' to yourself, because we both know better."

Before she could stop herself, she marched over to the table, placed her palms on his lean cheeks and, leaning down, kissed him for all she was worth. His firm lips immediately molded to hers, and when she traced them with the tip of her tongue it took very little coaxing to get him to allow her entry. Treating him to the same delightful exploration that he had treated her to each time he'd kissed her, Mariah stroked and teased his inner recesses until a groan rumbled up from deep in his chest. Only then did she raise her head to stare into his dark blue eyes. She might have laughed at his startled expression if she hadn't still been so frustrated with him.

"And you want to know something else, cowboy?" She didn't wait for him to respond. "I wanted to kiss you and I'm not one tiny bit sorry that I did. The only difference between us is that I readily admit that I want to kiss you until your boots fly off and a whole lot more."

When she turned to walk away, his voice sounded strained when he asked, "Where are you going?"

"I have things I need to do," she said as she walked

toward the pantry on shaky legs to resume putting things on the shelves.

He cleared his throat. “You can’t just kiss me like that and then walk away.”

“Why not?” she asked, turning to give him a pointed look. “That’s what you do.”

Before he had a chance to say anything else, she went into the pantry and, picking up a couple of boxes of snack crackers, stared at the labels without really seeing them. She had never done anything like that in her entire life. But it was time to treat Mr. Jaron Lambert to a dose of his own medicine. If he could kiss her and walk away as if it meant nothing, so could she. And if he thought he was going to convince her there was nothing between them, he was sadly mistaken. She might not be as experienced as he was, but she wasn’t that naive. There was something holding him back, and she wasn’t even contemplating trying to find another job until she discovered what it was.

Several hours later, Mariah put bags of noodles and pasta in lined sea-grass baskets and placed them on the shelves. Standing back, she proudly surveyed the labels she’d made and how organized everything looked.

“Don’t worry about making supper tonight,” Jaron said, causing her to jump.

“I wish you’d stop doing that,” she said, catching her breath.

“Do what?” he asked, looking puzzled.

“Sneaking up on me like that,” she retorted. Lost in thought, she hadn’t realized he had come back into the house again.

"I'll try to make more noise from now on," he said, smiling. "I wanted to tell you not to worry about making supper tonight. After I take a quick shower, I'll drive over to Beaver Dam and get a couple of steak dinners for us."

"Why? I thought part of my job description is to cook your meals," she said, frowning.

"You've worked hard all afternoon getting the pantry organized and all this food put away," he said, leaning one shoulder against the door frame as he crossed his arms over his wide chest. "You have to be tired. You can start cooking tomorrow."

"Suit yourself," she said, breathing a little easier as he turned to leave.

At least Jaron buying dinner would give her one more night without having to prepare a meal. He was going to learn soon enough that she had no idea what she was doing in a kitchen, and the longer she could put that off, the better.

Walking back into the kitchen, she watched him disappear down the hall to go upstairs. She was going to do her best and try to make things that he could actually eat. But she wasn't overly confident that would happen for a while. The poor man thought he had hired a woman who could make delicious meals with little or no effort like her sister. He had no idea that Mariah hadn't been born with the cooking gene.

"Hey, Jaron! We didn't expect to see your sorry hide in here tonight."

When Jaron turned to see who was calling to him, he

groaned. He hadn't expected to see two of his brothers at the Broken Spoke either when he went to pick up his and Mariah's supper. But sure enough, there were Ryder McClain and T. J. Malloy sitting at a table toward the back of the room, grinning at him like a couple of fools.

Giving his order for the steak dinners and a bottle of beer to the bartender, Jaron took his beer and walked over to sit down in one of the empty chairs at their table. "I assume I'm doing the same thing you two are doing. Along with this beer, I just ordered a couple of steak dinners for supper."

T.J. grinned as he cut into the steak in front of him. "A couple? You must be real hungry."

"And you're doing carryout? I'd say you're going to be entertaining a lady tonight," Ryder speculated, laughing.

"Anyone we know?" T.J. asked without missing a beat.

Jaron could have kicked himself for mentioning he had ordered two dinners. He should have known that his brothers would want to know who would be eating the other steak.

"I hired a housekeeper," Jaron said, hoping to avoid an inquisition. "She spent the day shopping and stocking the pantry. I figured I'd give her a break and have her start cooking tomorrow."

He watched T.J. and Ryder glance at each other for a moment before their gazes swung back to him. "Okay, what is it that you aren't telling us?" Ryder asked. "And don't try saying there isn't something, because we know you better than that. A seasoned housekeeper would be able to juggle grocery shopping and making supper with her eyes closed."

Jaron had wanted to wait until he and his brothers were all together to tell them that he had hired Mariah to be his housekeeper. He knew they were all going to needle him to death for details, and if he waited until they were together he would only have to endure their questions and comments once and get it over with. But it didn't appear that was going to happen.

He took a deep draw on his beer bottle before he set it down and met his brothers' suspicious gazes head-on. "I hired Mariah."

T.J. choked on the piece of steak he had just put in his mouth. Reaching over, Ryder pounded on T.J.'s back several times without his piercing gaze wavering from Jaron's. "How the hell did that happen? And when?"

"About a week ago, I came here for supper and Mariah walked in," Jaron said. Explaining what had happened with the hapless Roy Lee and about her car breaking down, he finished, "Because it was late and Sam and Bria were down in Houston at the stock show, I took her home with me for the night."

"Any one of us would have done the same," Ryder agreed. "But how did you get from helping her with her car troubles to giving her a job?"

"Over breakfast the next morning, I found out that she had lost her position at the real estate management company and she couldn't afford rent because her roommate moved out." He carefully omitted the fact that if he hadn't felt so damned guilty over making love to her and taking her virginity the night before, he might not have even thought of offering her the job.

Recovered from choking on his steak, T.J. shook his head. "You're playing with fire, bro. Are you sure you can handle it and still keep up your 'I'm too old for her' line of bull?"

Ryder nodded. "You know damned good and well that girl has been moon-eyed over you for years and still is. Although for the life of me I'm beginning to wonder why."

"And you've had a thing for her almost as long," T.J. added. "Have you finally decided that you aren't Methuselah after all?"

"I'm still too old for her," Jaron insisted, stubbornly shaking his head.

"I never thought I'd be saying this, but you better not be leading her on, bro," Ryder warned. "I'd hate to have to kick your ass from here into the next county."

Jaron glared at this brother. "You know me better than that."

They might be irritating the hell out of him, but he wasn't the least bit surprised that T.J. and Ryder were cautioning him about playing with Mariah's affections. She was their sister-in-law's younger sister, and that made all of them protective of her. But it also went back to their days of growing up on the Last Chance Ranch. Besides the obvious talk about using protection if their hormones got the better of them, one of the first things their foster father had told them when they all started dating was to respect a woman and not to lead her on if there wasn't any chance of something working out between them.

But as he sat there staring at his brothers, Jaron couldn't help but feel guilty. By giving Mariah a job and moving her into his home, was he giving her hope where there was none? When he'd made love to her, he'd known that Mariah had assumed it was the beginning of a shift in their friendship, even though he had told her up front that he wasn't promising her anything beyond that one night. In trying to help her out with her employment problems, was he only hurting her more than he already had?

"I'd rather drop dead right here and now than ever hurt Mariah in any way," he said aloud.

"You sound like a man in love," T.J. observed, as if he was some kind of expert on the subject.

Grinding his teeth, Jaron shook his head. "I don't want to hurt anyone, except maybe you right now."

He wished whoever was working in the Broken Spoke's kitchen would get his steaks ready so that he could bid his brothers farewell and leave. He loved all of his brothers, but T.J. and Ryder were reminding him of the war he was waging within himself—a battle that Mariah wasn't doing a thing to help him win. That kiss she'd given him at lunch had damned near sent him into orbit and left him wanting her more than he ever wanted anything in his entire life.

"What's really stopping you with Mariah, Jaron?" Ryder pressed, nailing Jaron with a piercing look. "And let's try the truth this time. We all know the nine-year age difference has nothing to do with the reason you won't give in to your feelings for her."

Jaron loved his brothers and would lay down his life for any one of them. But the major drawback of having them know him so well was they all knew when he wasn't being entirely honest with them.

Taking a deep breath, Jaron stared at the droplets of condensation running down the beer bottle in his hand. "I care too much for her to saddle her with a past like mine."

"We all have pasts," T.J. reminded him. "We weren't sent to the Last Chance Ranch because we were little angels."

"T.J.'s right," Ryder said, nodding. "We all did things when we were young that we regret and aren't proud of. But we found women who love us for the men we became and overlooked the stupid mistakes we made when we were growing up. All you did was run away from foster homes. What the rest of us did to get our asses in trouble was a lot worse than that."

"I understand that," Jaron argued. "But this is Mariah. She deserves the best and I'm not it."

T.J. grunted. "Bro, that's the dumbest thing I think I've ever heard you say. Remember, Hank always told us that we can't change the past, so we might as well leave what we did to land us in trouble back there where it belongs and make the most of the future. And the last I knew, you had done that."

Ryder nodded. "There isn't one of us who thinks we're good enough for our wives. But there's not a day goes by that we don't thank the good Lord above the women disagree."

"In case you haven't noticed, that's the way Mariah feels about you, bro," T.J. said, finishing his steak. "She may not know what happened with your old man or why you ran away from every foster home they put you in, but she knows you have a past and she overlooks it because of the man you are today."

"I'll think about it," Jaron said to placate them. Maybe if they thought he was giving what they said some thought, they'd shut up and leave him alone.

"Now that we've covered what's happening in my life, let me ask you both something," Jaron said, deciding that a change of subject was in order. "Why are you here and not at home with your wives and kids?"

T.J. grinned. "The kids are playing while Summer helps Heather go through designs and options for decorating our new baby's nursery. Once Heather and I find out what we're having, we'll start painting and decorating with cowboys or ballerinas."

"They suggested we come here because they know we're pretty useless when it comes to that kind of thing," Ryder added, laughing.

When Jaron heard the bartender call his name, he breathed a sigh of relief. "It looks as if supper's ready," he said, rising to his feet. As an afterthought, he added, "I'd appreciate it if you'd keep Mariah's working for me to yourselves." He knew that both Ryder and T.J. would keep their mouths shut and respect his wishes.

Both of his brothers nodded their agreement. "You intend to tell the others when you and Mariah show up for Sam's birthday dinner?" Ryder asked, sitting back from the table.

"I figure it's easier to tell everyone at one time and get it over with, instead of having to be asked the same questions over and over," Jaron explained.

"You're probably right," Ryder agreed.

"See you next weekend," T.J. called as Jaron walked over to the bar to get the carryout he'd ordered.

After he paid for the food, Jaron walked out of the bar to his truck and drove back to the Wild Maverick Ranch. His brothers had brought up a couple of things that he needed to give some serious thought.

Although she didn't know what had happened to land him in the foster-care system and eventually get him sent to the Last Chance Ranch, Mariah had always known he had been a troubled kid. And T.J. was right about one thing—she didn't seem to care. Mariah accepted him for who he was now, as opposed to who he'd been back then.

But unlike his foster brothers, he had been labeled a problem because of what his father had done more than for running away from foster homes. Foster families didn't want a serial killer's son living with them—probably because they feared he would turn out like his old man. And the few who had opened their homes to him had made his life so miserable with their accusing looks and constant questions about his father and what he knew about the murders that Jaron had ended up taking off. The last time the authorities had found him, the caseworker had contacted Hank Calvert and it had turned out to be the luckiest day of Jaron's life.

Their foster father had stressed that Jaron and his foster brothers should view their time at the Last Chance Ranch as a fresh start and had helped all of them grow up to be productive, upstanding men. He'd counseled them with his sage advice, and for the most part they had moved on and left their troubles in the past. So why hadn't Jaron been able to do that as completely as the others? If he could find a way to come to terms with what had happened in his childhood, would he finally feel free to try having a relationship with Mariah?

As he parked his truck in the garage, he glanced over at Mariah's car. He wasn't sure what the answers were. And until he figured it out, it was best just to leave things the way they were.

"Thank you for dinner," Mariah said as she and Jaron walked into the family room to watch television after they ate. "It was delicious, but I'm positively stuffed."

The carryout food that he'd brought back from the Broken Spoke had been very good, but the portions had been double the size of those at any restaurant she'd ever been to and more than she could possibly eat. She hadn't even been able to take a bite of the delicious-looking apple pie he'd bought for their dessert. Knowing how much he loved it, she'd insisted he eat her slice as well as his own.

"You've eaten there before, haven't you?" he asked, reaching for the remote.

"The other night when my car broke down was the first time I've ever been in the place," she admitted.

"Normally when I'm in the area, I'm at one of your family's dinners or parties."

"Speaking of family dinners, we have one coming up," he said, turning the television to a popular crime show. "Next weekend we'll be getting together for Sam's birthday."

"I'm looking forward to it," she said, slipping off her shoes to curl up in the corner of the couch. "I haven't seen the babies since Christmas." Bria and Sam's little boy was her only biological nephew, but she loved all of the foster brothers' children as if they were related by blood.

"It won't be long before there are two more." Jaron gave her a wary look. "We know Nate and Jessie are having a girl. I assume you think T.J. and Heather will have a girl, too."

Mariah smiled. "Of course." Every time one of the men's wives became pregnant, she had been positive the baby would be a girl, while Jaron had insisted it would be a boy. "I suppose you think Heather will have a boy."

"To tell you the truth, it really doesn't matter that much anymore." He shrugged. "I'd never been around little girls until Ryder and Summer had Katie. Now all it takes is one of her cute grins and I turn into a damned fool."

"That's the way I feel about all of them," she admitted. "The boys and Katie are all absolutely adorable and I couldn't love them more if I tried."

"Then, why do you keep insisting when one of the sisters-in-law learns she's pregnant that the baby is going to be a girl?" he asked, raising one dark eyebrow.

"You haven't figured it out yet?" she asked, laughing.

Looking confused, he shook his head. "Why don't you let me in on what you think I should have figured out."

"I just like arguing with you," she answered, grinning.

"That's it?" When she nodded, he frowned. "Why?"

Leaning toward him, she whispered, "Because I wanted to get your attention."

"Well, you did that." The lines on his forehead deepened. "I thought you were pissed off at me most of last year after I mentioned that I was right when Lane and Taylor found out they were having a boy."

"No woman likes for a man to gloat on the rare occasion she's wrong," Mariah warned.

"So you *were* mad at me?" he asked.

"I wasn't happy, but I was more miffed than I was angry."

He grunted. "What's the difference?"

"Miffed is unhappy," she explained. "Angry is what I was last week when you went Neanderthal on that poor man and escorted me out of the Broken Spoke because you thought I was incapable of handling the situation myself."

"I'd do it again in a heartbeat if the need arose," he said stubbornly. "And if I were you, I wouldn't feel too sorry for old Roy Lee. He needed a lesson in what it means to respect a woman, and I had no problem giving him a crash course on the subject."

She wanted Jaron to admit what she had suspected all along—that his strong reaction to the situation had been because of her and not just his sense of gallantry. "You'd have done the same if it had been any other woman?" she pressed.

"It wasn't." He clamped his mouth shut and stared at her for a moment before he slowly nodded. "Probably."

"But it wasn't just any woman, was it?" she said, moving closer to him. She couldn't believe her audacity. But if she was going to get to the bottom of things, she had to start somewhere. "It was me."

"Yeah." He didn't look happy about his admission.

"You want to know what I think?" she whispered close to his ear.

He went as still as a marble statue. "You're going to—" he cleared his throat "—tell me no matter what I say, aren't you?"

"Of course." Kissing the side of his neck, she smiled when she felt him shudder. "You're fighting a losing battle, cowboy."

"Mariah, I don't think—" He stared at her as if he waged war within himself. He closed his eyes for a moment, then opened them and wrapped his arms around her. "Oh, hell, I give up."

Before she could ask what he meant, Jaron pulled her onto his lap and fused his mouth with hers. Bringing her arms up to his wide shoulders, she held on to his solid strength as she kissed him back.

Tiny sparkles of light danced behind her closed eyes as his lips moved over hers, and when he coaxed her to allow him entry, she couldn't think of anything she wanted more than for him to deepen the kiss. At the first touch of his tongue to hers, a warmth like nothing she'd ever felt before settled in the most feminine part of her. Apparently he was experiencing the same kind of heat, because there was no denying the evidence of his hard arousal pressing insistently against the side of her hip.

Keeping his arms wrapped tightly around her, he shifted them to a more comfortable position and Mariah found herself stretched out on the couch with Jaron lying partially on top of her. With one of his thighs nestled snugly at the apex of her legs, desire streaked through her veins and caused a flutter of anticipation deep in the pit of her stomach. She wanted him, hadn't stopped wanting him since the night they made love. With sudden clarity, she knew she always would.

As he continued to explore her with a tenderness that robbed her of breath, he moved his hand from her shoulders down to cup her breast. The delicious sensation of his gentle touch as he teased the tip with the pad of his thumb caused her to feel as if her insides had been turned into hot wax. When he broke the contact to nibble kisses down the column of her throat to her collarbone, the tiny moan she'd been holding back escaped her parted lips.

"Does that feel good?" he asked as his lips skimmed her sensitive skin.

"It feels…amazing," she gasped.

"We shouldn't be doing this, Mariah," he said against her sensitive skin.

Placing her palms on either side of his face, she raised his head to meet her determined gaze. "I swear, if you stop…I'll never speak to you…again," she warned breathlessly.

His low chuckle sent a wave of energy to her core and she pressed herself more fully into him. As he continued to tantalize the tight peak through the layers of her clothing, Mariah shivered from the feel of his hard arousal against her thigh. He wanted her as much as she wanted him.

"I have something that I need to go check on down at the barn, darlin'," he said suddenly, sounding as if he had run a marathon. Getting up from the couch, he pulled her up to stand in front of him and softly kissed her forehead. "I'll be back a little later," he added, stepping away from her.

"After you cool off?" she asked point-blank.

He stared at her a moment before he silently nodded.

"Jaron, I want you to do something for me while you're out in the barn," she said as she brushed her hair from her eyes.

"What's that?"

"I want you to think about what I told you earlier," she replied, picking up her shoes to go upstairs. "You're fighting a battle you can't win. You can deny it all you want, but you want me as much as I want you and this is going to continue to happen as long as I'm living here." She shook her head. "And unless you fire me, I'm not going anywhere."

"I'm not firing you," he said without a moment's hesitation.

"Then, I suggest you come to terms with what's going on between us," she advised. "Because there's always been more than just friendship, and we both know it."

Five

After a miserable night, Jaron waited until the star-filled sky gave way to the pearl-gray light of dawn before he finally lost hope of getting any sleep and sat up on the side of his bed. Mariah had given him a lot to think about yesterday evening—as if having her around all the time hadn't been the *only* thing on his mind for the past week.

Resting his forearms on his knees, he stared down at his loosely clasped hands. Between what she had told him and what his brothers had mentioned about her knowing and not caring that there was some kind of trouble in his background, he had given serious thought to the possibilities, as well as the consequences.

There had been something going on between him and Mariah for several years. But whether she could accept his past or not, he wasn't sure he ever would. The stigma of being the son of someone the world considered to be pure evil wasn't something that went away that easily, and he had no intention of bringing that kind of repulsive reality into her life.

Unfortunately, it was becoming impossible to resist the temptation of having Mariah with him all the time and keep his hands to himself. He would like nothing more than to be free to hold her to him, kiss her until they both gasped for air and make love to her for as long as she wanted to stay with him. And she wasn't helping him to resist those needs. She'd let him know in more ways than one that she wanted that, too.

But he had to think of what was best for her and put that ahead of his own desires. She might not think his past was a problem, but he knew better. When he was young he'd had too many people look at him as if they thought he might murder them in their sleep once they learned who his father was. That wasn't something he would ever forget, nor was it anything he wanted Mariah to even consider. He hoped she never learned the revolting secrets he tried so hard to protect her from. He couldn't bear the thought of seeing the disillusionment in her eyes if she ever found out.

Jaron sighed heavily. He should probably fire her and send her on her way. But she needed the job and it was the only way he could think of to help her without hurting her pride or pissing her off to the point of her never speaking to him again.

Now, if he could just figure out a way to keep his hands to himself…

When he heard her close her bedroom door and start down the stairs, he abandoned his troubling thoughts, took a quick shower and got dressed. She would have breakfast ready soon and he had a full day's work ahead of him repairing fence with his men. Besides, there was no sense wasting time thinking about things that he couldn't change.

As he pulled on his boots, a keening wail suddenly split the air, raising the hair on the back of his neck and sending an icy chill straight up his spine. Jumping up from the bench at the end of the bed, Jaron ran out into the hall and headed for the stairs. While the smoke alarm screeched relentlessly, the acrid smell of something burning stung his nostrils and caused his eyes to water.

When he reached the kitchen, he immediately looked for Mariah. She was frantically opening cabinet doors, and he assumed she was looking for something to put out the fire. Fairly certain she was all right, he reached into the cabinet under the sink, pulled out the fire extinguisher and, removing the pin, aimed the hose at the flaming skillet on the ceramic stove top. As soon as he was sure the blaze was out, he went straight to the screaming smoke detector and removed the battery to stop the incessant noise.

"Are you all right?" he asked, going over to put his arm around her shoulders to guide her out onto the back porch.

Coughing, she nodded. "I'm okay, but I'm afraid breakfast is going to be late."

He hugged her close for a moment to reassure himself she was okay, then released her to reach for the door. "Stay here and catch your breath while I go open the windows to air out the kitchen."

When he returned, she was standing there shivering with her arms wrapped around her waist. He wasn't sure if she was cold or if she was having a nervous reaction to the fire. It didn't matter. Without giving it a second thought, he drew her to him to keep her warm.

"It's okay, darlin'," he said, gently rubbing her back. "All that matters is that you weren't hurt." When she nodded, he asked, "What was in the skillet?"

"I was trying to fry a couple of eggs, but they suddenly burst into flames," she answered, holding on to him as though he was her lifeline. "I think the oil might have been too hot."

He couldn't help but chuckle. "You may have just come up with a new recipe. I don't think I've ever heard of eggs flambé before."

"I suppose there's something I should tell you about my ability to cook," she said, her voice muffled from her face being buried in his chest.

"I'm listening," he said, doing his best not to laugh. He had a good idea what she was about to tell him.

"I don't know the first thing about cooking unless it's reading the back of a box to find out how many minutes to program the timer on a microwave," she admitted.

"But that apple pie you made for my birthday a couple of years ago tasted great," he reminded her.

"If Bria hadn't stood beside me and told me step by step what to do, it wouldn't have been edible." She shook her head. "I should have told you I can't cook."

"Oh, I kind of got that cooking might not be in your skill set when the smoke alarm went off. And if that hadn't tipped me off, I think the blazing skillet would have." Using his finger to lift her chin so their gazes met, he grinned. "Until a few minutes ago, I'd never seen black eggs."

Her cheeks turned pink. "I'm much better at business management."

"Let's go back inside," he suggested when she shivered against him. The weather was colder than normal for February, and he wouldn't be at all surprised if they were in for some kind of frozen precipitation.

Once they were back in the kitchen, Mariah scraped the charred eggs into the garbage disposal and put the skillet in sudsy water to soak while he closed the windows. "Would you like some toast for breakfast?" she asked, her voice a bit subdued. "I know I can make that."

He shook his head. "I'll just take a cup of coffee."

"I was going to ask you about that," she said, eyeing the coffeemaker as if it might bite her. "I normally waited until I got to work to have my morning coffee. The office had one of those makers that used the little individual cups."

All things considered, he probably shouldn't find her lack of kitchen knowledge amusing. But he did. "Making coffee is pretty easy. I'll show you what to do so you can make it tomorrow morning." Once he showed her how to get the coffeemaker started, he got two mugs from the cabinet and poured them both a cup when it finished brewing.

"Thank you," she said, adding creamer to her coffee.

Walking over to the table, she slumped into one of the chairs. “I thought I would ask Bria to show me a few simple things to make, but I haven’t had the chance to go over there yet.”

“Don’t worry about it.” He sat down beside her, then reached over to cover her hand with his. “If you don’t mind, I think I’m going to change your job description.”

“To what?” she asked, looking as though she expected the worst. “Unemployed?”

“No.” He smiled. “In light of recent events, I think it would be in both of our best interests to move you into a position that you’re more familiar with. How would you like to take over as ranch manager?”

“As long as it doesn’t involve getting near a stove, I’m sure I can do the job,” she said, sounding relieved. “But what are you going to do for a housekeeper and cook?”

“I think the first item on your agenda as ranch manager should be to hire someone who has a little more experience in the kitchen,” he teased, taking a sip of his coffee.

She smiled sheepishly. “If you want to eat more than burned offerings, that probably wouldn’t be a bad idea.”

He told her where to find the ranch files on his computer and gave her his password. “If you have time, you can familiarize yourself with the ranch records today. I’ll stick around the house tomorrow so that we can discuss what I have planned and set goals to make it happen.”

With a degree in ranch management, he could run the Wild Maverick with his eyes closed. But he had promised her a job and he wasn’t going back on his word.

"I think I already have someone in mind for the housekeeping position," Mariah said, looking thoughtful. "She used to work for me at the real estate management office and when we found out we no longer had jobs, she mentioned trying to find something closer to Stephenville, where her son and his family live."

"Can she cook?" he asked, grinning at her over the rim of his coffee mug.

She made a face at him. "Reba May is almost as good a cook as Bria," she answered proudly. "She used to do the cooking for all of our office parties and everything she made was delicious. I'll give her a call a little later and see if she's interested."

"It sounds as though you have it under control."

"If she's interested in the job would you like to meet her before I hire her?" she asked.

"I trust your judgment." He set his cup on the table and checked his watch. "I need to get down to the barn. I'm helping my men repair that stretch of fence in the south pasture today."

"Will you be back for lunch?" she asked. "I may not know how to cook, but I can make a sandwich for you."

When she nibbled on her lower lip, he barely managed to hold back a groan. She wasn't trying to be provocative, but that didn't lessen the effect her action had on him.

He shook his head as he rose to his feet to take his coffee cup to the sink. "When we're working out in the pastures, the bunkhouse cook always packs lunch for us." Giving in to the overwhelming urge to kiss her, he walked back to the table, pulled her up from the chair and, wrapping his arms around her waist, drew her to him. "And don't worry about supper. I think it would be a good idea to eat out this evening."

She laughed. "Where's your sense of adventure, cowboy?"

"I think I used that up when you tried to cook breakfast," he said, unable to stop himself from pressing his mouth to hers. Giving her a kiss that left them both breathless, he motioned toward the door. "The guys are waiting on me."

"Thank you, Jaron," she said softly.

He frowned. "What for?"

"For not firing me." She kissed the exposed skin at the open collar of his chambray shirt. "I'll see you later this afternoon."

Nodding, Jaron quickly turned, grabbed his wide-brimmed hat from a peg beside the door and walked out of the house before he changed his mind about helping his men mend the fence in the south pasture. So much for the pep talk he'd given himself when he first got out of bed. It had taken less than half an hour and he'd already reverted to kissing her first and thinking about it later.

Mariah had been right about a couple of things. There was a lot more going on between them than ever before, and it appeared he was definitely fighting a losing battle. He should tell her it would be better if she found another job. But as much hell as he'd gone through the past week, he still didn't want her to leave. Just the thought of her leaving caused a knot the size of a basketball to form in his gut.

Jaron took a deep breath as he walked across the yard toward the barn. He felt as if he had jumped off a cliff into the great unknown. But there was no way to turn back the clock. It appeared that when he'd made love to Mariah, he had started something that couldn't be stopped. And, God help him, he wasn't sure he even wanted to try.

Mariah closed the files on Jaron's computer and couldn't help but be very pleased with herself. She had not only reviewed all of the ranch files and felt ready to discuss goals for the ranch with Jaron tomorrow, she'd hired her former employee to take over the housekeeping and cooking duties at the Wild Maverick Ranch. Reba May had jumped at the job offer because of the close proximity to her son and his family, as well as the idea of being able to make a living doing what she loved—cooking. That was enough to make Mariah feel a lot better after the disaster with breakfast that morning. But when she talked to Reba May and learned that the woman had won the state fair pie-making contest with an apple pie, Mariah had been thrilled with her decision to hire the woman. Given his love of apple pie, she was fairly confident Jaron would be happy with her choice, as well.

As she sat there patting herself on the back for a job well done, her cell phone rang. Checking the caller ID, she smiled when she saw the call was from Bria.

"How is my favorite sister?" Mariah asked cheerfully.

"I'm your only sister," Bria answered drily. "That makes me the favorite by default."

"You sound tired." Mariah leaned back in Jaron's desk chair. "Has that sweet little nephew of mine been running you ragged?"

"Not any more than usual." Bria sighed. "I've been battling a stomach bug for the past week that I just can't seem to shake."

"Is there anything I can do to help?" Mariah asked, immediately concerned. "If you need me, I can watch little Hank so you can get some rest." Although Bria and Sam were more than financially able to hire a nanny to help with the toddler, Bria was a hands-on mother and loved every minute of it. She wouldn't even discuss having help with her son.

"Thank you, but he's been an angel since I got sick," Bria said, her voice reflecting her motherly love. "And speaking of my little man, he's due to wake up from his nap soon, so I'll have to make this quick. The reason I'm calling is about Sam's birthday dinner. Since I haven't felt well, Taylor is going to have the celebration at her and Lane's ranch a week from this Sunday."

Taylor Donaldson had worked as a personal chef before moving to Texas and had been helping Bria with all of the family get-togethers since marrying Lane. But it concerned Mariah that Bria might have something more serious than the stomach flu. She'd never known her sister not to cook Sam's birthday dinner herself.

"Have you been to a doctor?" Mariah asked. "Maybe there's something he can give you to help you get over this."

"I have an appointment tomorrow," Bria answered. "But I'm sure it's nothing to worry about. I just wanted to let you know about the change in plans."

"I'll be there," Mariah said, careful not to mention the word *we*. Apparently Jaron hadn't mentioned anything to his brothers about her working for him. If he had, she knew her sister would have questioned her about it. Besides, she fully intended to tell Bria about losing her job and moving to the Wild Maverick when she saw her the day of Sam's birthday dinner. Some things were just better discussed in person. "Let me know what you find out after you see the doctor, and if you change your mind about me watching little Hank, don't hesitate to let me know."

"I will," Bria promised. "I'll see you a week from Sunday. Love you."

"Love you more, sis," Mariah said before ending the call. Since their parents had been taken from them so unexpectedly, they never parted without telling each other how they felt.

Mariah left Jaron's office and headed upstairs to take a shower and change. He would be back soon from working with his men and she wanted to be ready to go out for dinner.

She briefly wondered why he hadn't told his brothers about hiring her, but she had been just as reluctant to share her change of employment with Bria. Maybe Jaron was trying to avoid a barrage of questions, the same as she was.

Mariah loved her sister with all her heart, but Bria could be the overly protective big sister at times and especially where Jaron was concerned. It wasn't that Bria didn't trust him to be anything but a perfect gentleman. Mariah was certain that her sister trusted all of Sam's foster brothers without hesitation.

But Bria had known how Mariah felt about Jaron from the time they'd been introduced. Bria also knew that Jaron had never led her on or given her any reason to believe that he viewed her as anything but Bria's younger sister. Mariah was certain that if Bria got wind of her working at the Wild Maverick Ranch, she would feel compelled to caution Mariah about reading more into the situation than was really there.

Of course, her sister didn't know the entire story and Mariah had no intention of telling her. What happened between two consenting adults was no one else's business, and as far as Mariah was concerned that was the way it was going to stay. She would listen to Bria's concerns and even answer the questions she could without revealing the personal aspects of her stay at the Wild Maverick Ranch. Beyond that, no one else needed to know what went on between her and Jaron.

The following day, Jaron sat across the desk from Mariah, wondering how he was going to keep his mind on ranch business when all he could think about was taking her upstairs and making love to her. When they'd gone out for supper the night before, he'd had the same problem concentrating. Mariah had been extremely enthusiastic about the woman she'd hired to take over the housekeeping position and told him all about her. He couldn't recall a single thing she'd said other than the woman's name was Reba something or other and that she wouldn't be starting until the first of next month.

Fortunately, when they returned to the ranch, he'd received a call from his ranch foreman to tell him the calving season had started early. A couple of the prize-winning heifers he'd bought had gone into labor, and after seeing Mariah into the house, he'd walked down to the calving shed to check on them. He was sure his men could have taken care of the bovine maternity watch, but he'd used the excuse to escape what he knew now to be the inevitable. He and Mariah would be making love again—and soon.

He took a deep breath as he came to terms with that. He had reached the end of his rope and no amount of telling himself he was doing what was right had worked. His best efforts to fight his growing need for her had failed miserably and it was past time that he gave up and admitted it.

But as much as he burned for her, he was determined that it would be different than when they made love before. When he loved her again, it wouldn't be rushed the way it had been the night he'd brought her home with him from the Broken Spoke. Mariah deserved to be loved slowly, to be cherished in a way that let her know how special she was. She deserved the pampering and romance that had been lacking the first time he'd loved her.

"Are you listening to me, Jaron?" Mariah asked, looking impatient.

"Sorry." He cleared his throat. "I was thinking about something else."

"That's apparent," she said, laughing. "I asked you if you intend to raise nothing but free-range cattle."

He nodded. "That's the plan. There's a big market for drug and supplement free beef, and the demand for it is growing."

"What about the breed?" she asked, making notes on her electronic tablet. "Are you going to remain a purebred Brangus operation or will you be introducing other breeds into the herd?"

"I'm sticking with the Brangus," he said, amused by her questions. She'd obviously researched her job and was trying to learn all she could about being a ranch manager.

"From everything I've read about them, they're a pretty popular breed of beef cattle," she agreed, adding to her notes.

"Brangus are a cross between Brahman and Black Angus cattle and have the best traits of both." He shrugged. "They yield a good-tasting, high-quality grade of lean beef like the Angus and are more disease resistant and better suited to the Texas climate like the Brahman."

"That makes sense." She frowned as she looked directly at him. "You know your breed and why you chose it and you have a clear goal to keep the herd free-range. Why do you need me to be the ranch manager when you have all of this worked out and could easily manage the ranch yourself?"

"Because I'm a cowboy at heart, darlin'." Giving in to the heat flowing through his veins, he rose from his chair, rounded the desk and, scooping her up into his arms, sat down in the armchair and settled her on his lap. "You can take care of managing the ranch while I'm out working with my hired hands."

As she stared at him, he felt as if he could easily lose himself in her emerald eyes. "Jaron, I've never been good at playing games."

He didn't even try to pretend he didn't know what she was referring to. "I've never been any good at that, either, Mariah."

"Then, why have you been running hot and cold for the past week and a half?" she asked pointedly. "You pull me in and then push me away and I want to know why."

"I'm sorry." He kissed her soft, perfect lips. "I've been trying to do what I thought was best for you, but just having you here with me has undermined all of my good intentions."

To his surprise, she grinned. "In other words, I was right. You've been fighting a losing battle."

"Yeah, I guess I have," he admitted, smiling back at her.

"I'm glad you finally came to your senses and realized that. So where do we go from here?" she asked, her expression turning serious. "Are you going to tell me why you made love to me and then shut me out as if I was nothing more than a one-night stand? Or are you going to push me away again?"

"You don't pull any punches, do you?"

She shook her head. "I told you, I don't play games."

He knew he should tell her everything and wish her the best in life as he watched her walk away from him.

Instead, he took a deep breath and told her as much as he could without going into the revolting part about his father.

"After my mother died, I didn't have anyone who cared about me," he said, barely able to remember the woman who had given him life. "I learned early on that I always came up lacking in one way or another and it was easier not to count on anyone being there for me or caring what happened to me. It wasn't until I was sent to the Last Chance Ranch because I kept running away from the foster homes they put me in that I learned what having a family meant."

"Is that why you've always been more quiet and reserved than your brothers?" she asked softly. "You wanted to avoid rejection?"

"It's easier being a loner than setting yourself up for failure," he said, nodding. There was some truth in her assumption, and certainly where she was concerned.

"Do you think you're ready to take a chance now?" she asked, looking cautious.

He wasn't going to lie to her, but he couldn't tell her that wasn't the only reason holding him back, either. "Darlin', I doubt I'll ever be able to get past that part of my life," he said honestly. "But when we made love, it wasn't just a meaningless one-night stand and I don't ever want you to think it was." Wrapping his arms around her, he gave her a quick kiss. "Like I told you the other night, I can't offer you anything beyond the here and now. But that doesn't mean I don't want you." He knew she wasn't happy with his answer and he couldn't say he blamed her. "I know that isn't fair to you and I'll understand if you decide you want to cut your losses and leave."

"No, I'm not leaving." She gave him a smile that caused his heart to stall, then start beating like a war drum. "I'm looking forward to seeing what it's like to manage a working cattle ranch."

"It's a nice day," he said, setting her on her feet. He stood up and put his arms around her. "What do you say we get out of the house and take a ride around the ranch so you can see what you're going to be managing?"

"Ride as in on a horse?" she asked, looking a little apprehensive.

He nodded. "Is that a problem?"

"It might be, considering I don't know how to ride," she said, laughing.

"You can't live on a ranch without learning to ride a horse," he teased. "We'll ride double today and I'll start teaching you next week when we have a little more time."

"I'll get my jacket," she said, pulling away from his arms.

"Meet me down at the barn," he said as he watched her climb the stairs. "I'll go ahead and get my horse saddled."

As he left the house to walk down to the barn, Jaron felt better about telling Mariah what he could regarding his background. By no stretch of the imagination had he been transparent about his past, but his explanation seemed to be enough, at least for now.

He had no doubt the day would come when she'd

want the whole story. But he intended to put that off as long as he could and enjoy what time he had with her.

Ten minutes later, Jaron swung up into the saddle, then lifted Mariah up to sit across his thighs. Putting his arms around her, he picked up the reins and, nudging Chico into a slow walk, guided the horse out of the feedlot. They hadn't ridden fifty feet from the barn before he was wondering what the hell he'd been thinking. Her delightful little bottom rested snugly against his groin, causing him to react in a very predictable way.

He had considered putting Mariah on one of the older, more docile mares, but decided against it. She wouldn't have known what she was doing or how to control the animal on the outside chance the horse got spooked. For her safety and his peace of mind, he would rather teach her to ride in the round pen, where he had more control over her first lesson than out in an open field.

"Is that a creek up ahead?" she asked, seemingly oblivious to his predicament.

He did his best to ignore the signals his body was sending him and concentrated on answering her questions about the ranch. "There are two creeks," he said, shifting in the saddle to relieve some of the mounting pressure. "One here in the south pasture and one winding from the northeast to the western side of the property."

"Good for watering livestock," she commented. He found her determination to learn all she could about managing the ranch and all of the research she'd obviously done on the subject endearing.

He kissed her temple. "That's one of the reasons I bought this place. Besides being close to all of my brothers, it had good pastures for grazing and adequate water for the herds."

As they continued the tour of his ranch, he answered a good two dozen questions or more about the property, and by the time they turned back toward the house an hour or so later, he felt that Mariah was going to be a great ranch manager. Her questions and observations had been insightful and she'd even offered a couple of suggestions on the goals they had set.

But the ride was starting to take a real toll and he decided it was time to head back to the house before he lost what little sense he had left. Every time Mariah moved, the pressure building in the region south of his belt buckle increased, and he had enough adrenaline pumping through his veins to lift a tractor.

"I'll have to finish showing you around the northern part of the Wild Maverick another day," he said, deciding he'd had about all he could take. "It's going to start getting dark soon."

"I've really enjoyed seeing your land," she said, resting her head against his shoulder. "Thank you for showing me around."

"I'm glad you had a good time," he said as they rode into the ranch yard. "This spring we'll have to get the cook to pack us a lunch and go for a picnic down by one of the creeks."

"Can we go fishing?" she asked, sitting up to look over her shoulder at him. "When we were little, our dad took me and Bria fishing a few times. The best I can remember, we played in the water more than we fished, but we had a lot of fun."

He nodded. "When the real estate agent was showing me around the property last fall, he said that the creeks had catfish and bluegill."

"I wouldn't know the difference," she said, laughing. "But I'm looking forward to it."

She sounded as if she really meant it, and Jaron decided right then and there that whatever hell he'd gone through showing her around his ranch had been more than worth it. He might not be able to assure her that there would be a tomorrow for them, but he could do everything in his power to make her happy for as long as they were together.

And come hell or high water, that was exactly what he was going to do.

Six

When Mariah walked into her closet after her shower, she started going through clothes, wondering what on earth she was going to wear for her night out with Jaron. A few days ago, when they'd returned from their ride around the ranch, he'd been called away to help his men in the calving sheds and she hadn't seen a lot of him the rest of the week. He had apologized and explained that calving season ran for several weeks, and because the majority of the cows having calves now were first-time mothers, they had to be watched more closely for signs of trouble during the birthing process. But when he'd come in earlier than usual this afternoon, he'd surprised her by telling her to dress up for dinner because he had something special planned for Valentine's Day.

Pushing back hangers as she tried to decide on a

dress, Mariah smiled. Since their talk a few days ago, Jaron had been more at ease and now took every opportunity he could to touch her or take her in his arms for kisses that left her head spinning. And she loved every minute of it.

She knew it wasn't a commitment or even the promise of one. But it did give her hope.

It might be foolish of her to think that Jaron could eventually overcome the sadness and abandonment of his childhood. And her intuition was telling her that there were more problems in his past than what he had told her. But he had shared part of it, and that was a start. Maybe one day, he would be able to tell her all of what he had been through and the reason behind his being sent to the Last Chance Ranch. She realized that she could very well be deluding herself and opening the door for a broken heart if he couldn't. But she would never know if she didn't take that leap of faith. And not giving them a chance was simply not an option.

With her mind made up to give him the time to fully trust her with his secrets, she turned her attention back to finding something to wear. When she pushed a black cocktail dress aside to reveal the simple red minidress she'd worn the night Jaron had brought her home with him from the Broken Spoke, she grinned. He'd really seemed to like the formfitting knit jersey fabric and drop shoulders. And since it was a beautiful dark red with a little bit of shimmer to it, it would be perfect for a Valentine's Day dinner.

With her mind made up to wear exactly what she'd worn the night he'd made love to her, she slipped the dress from the hanger and grabbed her black spike heels from the built-in oak shoe rack. Walking back into the bedroom, she placed them on the bed, then opened the dresser drawer where she kept her lingerie. As she put on the matching strapless black lace-and-satin bra and panties, she hoped Jaron found them as irresistible this time as he had the first time he'd seen her in them.

Thirty minutes later, she walked out of the bedroom toward the stairs. Her makeup was in place, her hair was styled and she was ready for a night out with the sexiest man she'd ever known.

Her breath caught when she spotted the man who had captured her heart the first time she'd seen him waiting for her at the bottom of the winding staircase. Dressed in a long-sleeved white Oxford cloth shirt and dark blue jeans, Jaron looked amazing. When he looked up and saw her, the appreciation in his dark blue eyes and the smile on his handsome face caused her stomach to flutter and sent a wave of warmth coursing through her. If it was possible, he stole her heart all over again.

"You look absolutely beautiful," he said, taking her hand in his when she reached the bottom step.

She smiled. "You clean up pretty nice yourself, cowboy."

He gave her a kiss so soft and so tender it brought tears to her eyes. "I love this dress," he whispered close to her ear.

A shiver of anticipation coursed through her. "Are you going to tell me where we're going?" she asked, wondering if that throaty female voice was really hers.

"Not yet," he said, leading her down the hall. He

stopped just before they reached the kitchen. "Close your eyes."

"Jaron, what—"

He placed his index finger to her lips to silence her. "I want this to be a surprise," he said, kissing her bare shoulder.

Her skin tingled where his lips had been and she didn't think twice about doing as he commanded. "Don't let me walk into anything," she said, laughing breathlessly. As he put his arm around her waist to guide her and they continued on across the kitchen, she sensed that they weren't alone. "Jaron?"

"Just keep your eyes closed, darlin'."

Not wanting to ruin his surprise, she continued to allow him to lead her, and even with her eyes closed, she could tell they had entered the darkened sunroom. "May I open my eyes now?"

"Give me just a minute," he said, stepping away from her. She suddenly smelled the acrid scent of a lit match a moment before Jaron returned to her side. "You can open them now, Mariah."

The room was dark except for a lit single white taper in a gold candleholder sitting in the middle of a small round table along the south wall of windows. Two white china table settings sat across from each other on the red tablecloth, and when she looked up at the room's glass ceiling, the dark night sky outside was sprinkled with thousands of twinkling stars.

"Jaron, this is gorgeous," she said, turning to put her arms around his neck. "But who's in the kitchen?"

He laughed and, wrapping his arms around her waist,

kissed the tip of her nose. "The caterer and her assistant."

"How did you manage to pull all of this together in the short time I was upstairs?" she asked.

"Darlin', it takes me less than thirty minutes to get a shower, shave and put my clothes on," he said, grinning. "It takes you a good hour and a half to do whatever you do to get ready to go somewhere."

"Are you complaining?" she asked, raising one eyebrow.

"Hell no!" He gave her a kiss that curled her toes inside her four-inch heels. "I'd wait all day for the way you look tonight."

"That sounds like a line from a song," she said, laughing.

He shrugged as he led her over to the table. "I don't know if it is or not, but it's the truth." Holding her chair for her to sit down, he seated himself in the chair across from her. "I hope you don't mind not going out for the evening."

"Not at all," she said as the caterer's assistant approached the table with a bottle of champagne.

After the man filled crystal flutes with the sparkling wine and went back to the kitchen, Jaron reached across to cover her hand with his. "I didn't want to share you with anyone this evening."

His words and the warmth of his touch sent goose bumps shimmering over her skin. "I'm glad," she whispered as the waiter appeared again with their plates of food.

Sitting under the stars, they enjoyed a delicious dinner of prime rib, asparagus and rice pilaf. When they were finished, the waiter discreetly cleared the table. The chef joined them a few moments later carrying a silver tray filled with juicy chocolate-dipped strawberries. Thanking them for using the catering service, the woman bade them good-night before she and the waiter left.

"I couldn't have asked for a nicer evening," Mariah said as Jaron picked up one of the strawberries and held it to her lips. Taking a bite of the decadent dessert, she savored the mixed flavors of the tart berry with just the right amount of semisweet dark chocolate. "Thank you. This has been perfect."

He shook his head as he fed her the rest of the strawberry. "It's not over yet, darlin'."

"What else do you have planned?" she asked, marveling at his romantic gestures thus far.

"You'll see," he answered, smiling as he wiped a drop of strawberry juice from her lower lip.

Taking the tip of his finger into her mouth, she licked the droplet away and watched as his eyes darkened to navy. "I'm looking forward to finding out what other surprises you have in store for me," she said, feeling warmed all over by his heated gaze.

As they continued to stare at each other, the building tension between them was palpable and only broken briefly when he rose to his feet and walked over to a small control panel on the far wall. He pushed a button and the opening notes of a popular slow country song came from the speakers of the house audio system.

When he returned to the table, he held out his hand. "Could I have this dance, Mariah?"

"I thought you'd never ask," she said, placing her hand in his. She was well aware that he didn't care for dancing and had only made the gesture because he knew how much she loved it. Her heart swelled with emotion at his thoughtfulness.

He immediately took her in his arms, and as they swayed in time to the music, she felt surrounded by the sheer power of the man holding her close. She brought her arms up to his wide shoulders and tangled her fingers in his dark brown hair where it brushed the collar of his shirt, and stared up into the eyes of the man who had given her the most romantic, most memorable Valentine's Day of her life.

As they continued to hold each other, the song ended and another one began. Neither of them noticed. The steady beat of his heart against her breast and the evidence of his growing arousal nestled to her lower belly caused her to feel as if she would melt into a puddle at his booted feet. If she'd thought her need for him the night they made love was overwhelming, what she felt at that moment was all consuming.

"I want you, Mariah," he said, his voice low and intimate.

"And I want you," she said, feeling anticipation flow throughout her body. He kissed her and she felt as if her knees turned to jelly.

"Let's go upstairs," he suggested when he lifted his head.

Unable to find her voice, she simply nodded.

He turned to blow out the candle on the table, then put his arm around her shoulders and held her to his side as they walked out of the sunroom and went upstairs. They passed her bedroom and continued on down the hall to the master suite. Once they were inside and he closed the door behind them, Mariah wasn't at all surprised when he scooped her up into his arms and carried her to the bed.

"Why do you like carrying me?" she asked, kissing the column of his neck. "Is it an alpha male thing?"

He chuckled. "I hadn't really thought about it, but that might be." He set her on her feet beside the bed, then gently kissed her. "More likely it's because I can hold you closer and have easier access when I want to kiss you."

Mariah raised her hand to cup his jaw. "You won't get any complaints from me about that," she said, smiling.

"I know it's a little late to ask you this, but are you sure this is what you want, darlin'?" he asked, staring down at her.

"I've wanted you since we made love the first time, Jaron," she said seriously. "And I'm almost certain you've wanted me."

"Every minute of every day since," he admitted, nodding. He hesitated a moment before he added, "I still can't promise—"

She placed her finger to his mouth to silence him. "I'm not asking you for any kind of promises or declarations. All I want is to share the same beautiful experience with you that we had the first time we made love."

"I promise it will be better," he said, kissing her finger.

Moving her hand to touch the pulse beating at the base of his throat, she shook her head. "I don't see how that's possible."

"In that case, I guess I'll just have to show you," he said, slowly lowering his head.

When he captured her lips with his, Mariah knew in her heart that Jaron cared deeply for her. He might not even realize how much, but she did. No man had ever held her in his arms as if she were a rare and precious gift or kissed her as tenderly as he did. For now, that was enough for her.

As he continued to explore and tease her, she sighed from the sheer joy of being in his arms. Her pulse raced when he slipped his tongue between her parted lips and coaxed her into an erotic game of advance and retreat as he stroked and caressed.

All too soon, he eased away from the kiss to nibble his way along her jaw and down her throat to her collarbone. "Why don't we get out of these clothes so I can love you," he said, his smile reflecting his intention as he bent to pull off his boots and remove her high heels.

"I think that's an excellent idea," she agreed. She briefly wondered why he hadn't turned on the bedside lamp. But a dim light from the partially open door of the bathroom cast their silhouette on the closed drapes and she found it extremely romantic.

Forgetting about the light, she unbuttoned his cuffs, then reached for the button below his open shirt collar. "I want to touch those rippling abs of your again."

He laughed. "That's what turns you on about me? My abs?"

She grinned as she released first one button and then another. "And your pecs and your biceps and your quads and—"

"I get the idea," he interrupted when she released the button above his belt buckle.

Running her index finger along the top of it, she lightly grazed the warm skin just below his navel with her fingernail. "I also like your flat stomach and lean flanks."

He groaned when she slipped her finger beneath his waistband. "You're playing with fire, darlin'."

"You want me to stop?" she asked, glancing up at him as she tugged his shirt from his jeans.

His wicked grin warmed her all the way to her toes. "I didn't say that."

She unbuckled his belt and released the snap at the top of his fly. "What are you saying, cowboy?"

"For every action there's an equal reaction." He shuddered when she played with the tab of his zipper.

"I don't think that's exactly the way Newton's law of motion goes," she teased.

"When you get finished with your brand of torture, I'll show you." The promise in his dark blue eyes thrilled her.

"I'm looking forward to it," she said, trailing her fingernail down the metal closure holding him captive.

He suddenly took a step back. "Zippers can be dangerous to a man in my condition," he said, laughing as he eased the tab down. "I'd hate for one wrong move to ruin all of your fun."

"Aren't you having a good time?" she asked, loving their sexy banter.

"Oh, yeah." He leaned close to whisper in her ear. "But I'm going to have an even better time when I get to prove what I meant about Newton's law."

Mariah shivered with anticipation. "I'm looking forward to it."

When she placed her hands on his shoulders to brush his shirt away, her breath caught at the perfection of his broad chest and bulging biceps. "Your body is flawless."

"Like I told you before, looks can be deceiving," he said, shaking his head. Before she could ask what he meant, he shoved his jeans and boxer briefs down his legs, stepped out of them and kicked them aside. "You've got my engine firing on all cylinders and it's time for me to show you what I meant about that action/reaction thing."

As he brought his mouth down on hers, his hands came up to push her dress over her shoulders and down her arms. When it drifted to the floor around her feet, he held her gaze with his and slipped her panties over her hips and down her legs to join her dress on the floor. Once she stepped away from the pool of her clothing, Jaron unfastened her bra, tossed it aside and pulled her to his wide chest. The feel of her breasts against all those hard muscles caused her knees to wobble.

"You feel so damned good, Mariah," he said, burying his face in her hair.

If she could have found her voice, she would have

told him she felt the same way about him. But since words were beyond her capabilities, she nibbled kisses from the strong column of his neck to his collarbone then down to the thick pads of his pectoral muscles. He went completely still when she kissed one flat male nipple, then the other.

"You're trying to…give me a heart attack…aren't you," he said, sounding completely out of breath.

A feeling of feminine power coursed through her at the thought that she could instill that kind of desire in him. "I need you more now than you can possibly know, Jaron."

"I need you, too, darlin'." He took a deep breath. "Let's lie down while we still have the strength to get into bed."

Once they were stretched out on his king-size bed, he pulled her to him and kissed her with a passion that caused her to feel light-headed. When he broke the caress, he brushed his lips along her cheeks, her neck and the hollow behind her ear as he gently cupped her breast in his large palm. The delicious abrasion of his calluses on her sensitive skin sent tingles of excitement spiraling all the way to her feminine core.

Needing to touch him, to bring him the same degree of pleasure, she slowly skimmed her hand over his abs and taut stomach. When she felt the crisp hair below his navel, she traced the line with her finger until she found his persistent arousal.

She had no idea what she was doing, but as she measured his length and girth, a low groan rumbled up from deep in his chest. She took it as a positive sign that he was enjoying her exploration. But as she continued to learn his body, an impatience built deep inside her and she ached for him to make them one.

"Darlin', don't get me wrong," he said suddenly, catching her hand in his. "I love what you're doing. But if you keep that up, we're both going to be mighty disappointed."

"Then, why don't you do something to keep that from happening," she said, slightly shocked by her own boldness.

"Good idea." He gave her an encouraging smile. "I promise it won't hurt this time, Mariah," he said as he reached for a foil packet on the top of the bedside table.

When he had the protection in place, he rose above her and, taking her hand in his, helped her guide him to her. Her heart skipped a beat as he slowly moved forward and began to enter her. The exquisite fullness and the feeling of becoming one with the man who meant so much to her were overwhelming. She'd never felt more complete in her entire life than when they made love and she knew beyond a shadow of doubt that what she felt for Jaron was no longer the starry-eyed crush she'd had on him as a teenage girl. What she felt for him now went deeper and was far more real.

When his lower body rested against hers, he remained perfectly still. "Are you all right? There isn't any discomfort, is there?"

"I'm fine," she said, wrapping her arms around his neck. "Please make love to me, Jaron."

His gaze held hers as he began a slow rocking motion, and Mariah quickly lost herself to the wonderful feeling he was creating inside her. As the sensations began to build, she felt as if they were one body, one heart and one soul. She fought to prolong the connection between them as long as she could, but all too soon she felt her feminine muscles tighten as she approached the culmination they both sought.

Suddenly feeling as if a thousand stars had burst inside her, she was released from the delicious tension, and waves of intense pleasure flowed through every fiber of her being. As she floated back to reality, she felt Jaron's body surge inside her as he found his own satisfaction. When he collapsed on top of her, she kissed his shoulder and, wrapping her arms around him, held him to her as she reveled in the feeling that she was completely surrounded by him.

"I'm too heavy for you," he said, starting to lever himself off her.

Reluctant to let him go, she tightened her arms around him. "That was even more beautiful than the first time," she murmured against his shoulder.

"It's only going to get better each time we make love," he said, kissing her with such tenderness it brought tears to her eyes.

As he moved to her side, her fingers slid over his back and she felt several smooth ridges that she hadn't noticed the first time they made love. Her heart stalled when she remembered the scars on top of his shoulders that she'd asked about that night. He'd given her an excuse about all rodeo riders having their share of scars. But what she felt on his back didn't feel like anything that could have come from riding the rough stock.

"Jaron, could I ask you something?"

Gathering her to him, he kissed the top of her head. "What do you want to know, darlin'?"

With her head pillowed on his shoulder, she looked up at him in the semidarkness. "Are those scars on your back?"

His body stiffened and the smile on his face immediately disappeared. "Yes," he answered tightly.

She could tell by the shadows in his blue eyes that she'd asked him about something he'd just as soon forget. Placing her hand on his cheek, she caressed his jaw. "What happened, Jaron?"

"I don't want to talk about it," he said stubbornly.

"But—"

"You don't need to know," he said, cutting her off. There was an edge to his voice that warned her to drop the matter.

She stared at him for a moment, knowing the blemishes were tied into his reasons for thinking he wasn't right for her. "I'm sorry," she said softly. "I didn't mean to pry."

He closed his eyes a moment. When he opened them, he shook his head. "They don't matter. Let's forget about them and get some rest."

"Maybe I should go back to my room," she said, hating that she'd brought up a painful subject for him. The evening had been perfect until that point and she felt as if she'd ruined the intimacy between them.

His arms tightened around her. "I think you should stay right here."

Glancing up at him, she saw that the shadows in his

eyes were gone, and she knew as far as he was concerned the matter was closed. “All right.” She snuggled into his embrace. “But you have to promise to get me up early in the morning.”

“Why?”

“I need to do some laundry and I want to go over the list of supplies we need for your horses before I call the feed store to place an order for delivery,” she said, yawning.

When they fell silent, Mariah couldn’t stop thinking about what she’d discovered. She could only imagine what had taken place all those years ago and what Jaron had been through. He had mentioned that after his mother died no one had cared what happened to him, but she’d thought he was harboring the memory of a disillusioned child. Now she knew it was much more than that. It had been all too real.

It was clear that Jaron had suffered at the hands of someone cruel and heartless. She understood more now than ever before why he had always been quieter and more reserved than the other brothers from the Last Chance Ranch. He had been an abused child and he was still haunted by it.

Placing her arm over his wide chest, she held him close. Her heart ached at the thought of what he must have gone through as a child and, blinking back tears, she vowed not to ask him again about the scars on his back. At some point in time, if he felt ready to tell her what happened, she’d listen. But she’d rather die than dredge up such painful memories for him ever again.

But how would his unwillingness to share the rest

of what happened all those years ago—likely, the most traumatic events—affect their relationship? Would he eventually be able to open up and tell her the details of what he'd endured? Or would he try to keep them locked away from her and suffer in silence?

Mariah wasn't sure what the answers were or what obstacles she faced in trying to help him move past that part of his life. All she knew was that she had to be patient. Pressing him for the answers would only shut him down and she might never learn what happened.

She sighed as she felt herself start to fall asleep. Jaron needed her patience and understanding. Fortunately, she had an overabundance of patience where he was concerned. Otherwise, she wouldn't have waited seven years for him to finally realize they were meant to be together.

Seven

The following Sunday, as Jaron drove his truck along the road leading to the Lucky Ace Ranch, he glanced over at Mariah in the passenger seat beside him. Since asking about his scars after they made love, she hadn't mentioned them again. He knew she was still curious about what had made the marks, but if he told her how he got the lines crisscrossing his back, then he'd have to tell her about his sadistic father. That was sure to cause her to ask more questions that he wasn't about to answer.

The more he revealed about his past, the bigger the chance that she would either remember hearing about his father and the murders he'd committed or more likely, she would do an internet search and find out the whole sordid story. He felt safe that she hadn't done that already because of the judge ruling that he could take his mother's maiden name after his father's conviction. But just the thought of Mariah looking at him with fear and suspicion the way some of the foster families he'd been sent to live with had done made a knot the size of his fist form in his stomach.

"Have you told your brothers about hiring me to work at the ranch?" she asked, breaking into his disturbing thoughts.

They hadn't discussed when or what they were going to tell the rest of the family about her working at the Wild Maverick, but he suspected her reasons for keeping things on the down low were similar to his own. She looked a little uneasy and he felt just as apprehensive. He'd already gone through one interrogation with his brothers Ryder and T.J. He wasn't looking forward to another inquisition by the other three. And there wasn't a doubt in his mind that was exactly what was going to happen.

The entire family had known about Mariah's crush on him. And they weren't blind. They could tell he was just as attracted to her as she was to him. They'd also known that his insistence he was too old for her had evolved over the years from a valid reason into an excuse to keep her at arm's length. In the past few years, he'd endured their good-natured ribbing about asking Mariah out on a date, but if Ryder and T.J.'s reaction was any indication, they were also concerned that it might not work out between them. Or worse yet, that one or both of them would end up with a broken heart.

"I didn't have a choice about telling Ryder and T.J.,"

he admitted as he steered the truck onto the ranch road leading up to Lane and Taylor's house. "I ran into them the night I went to pick up our supper at the Broken Spoke. But I asked them to keep a lid on the news until we were all together."

"I had the chance to tell Bria when she called about the change in plans for Sam's party, but she wasn't feeling well and I didn't want to go into it," Mariah said, nodding.

Jaron could understand her reluctance. It was his guess that her sister would have the same concerns as his brothers, and if Bria wasn't feeling well, Mariah probably didn't want to worry her.

Of course none of them knew that he and Mariah weren't just employer and employee. Since they'd made love after their Valentine's Day dinner, she had moved into the master suite with him, and as far as he was concerned that was where she would stay for as long as she wanted.

A twinge of guilt once again settled across his shoulders. He didn't think he was leading her on. He'd made it clear that he wasn't making any promises, and she had told him she wasn't asking for any. But was it really that simple? How long would she be satisfied with that arrangement? For that matter, how long would he?

As he parked his truck by his brothers' pickups and SUVs, Jaron decided that he really didn't want to know the answers. He was afraid that if he knew for certain Mariah thought there was a chance something would come of their time together, he wouldn't have the strength to do the right thing for both of them and send her on her way.

"Time to face the family," he said, taking a deep breath as he got out of the truck and walked around to open the passenger door for her.

"I...um... I'm not telling Bria or the other women about the nature of our relationship," she stated. "Only that I'm working at your ranch."

He nodded. "It's nobody's business but ours."

"I agree." Her smile caused his heart to thump hard against his rib cage. "Besides, I like the intimate feeling of it being our little secret."

"I feel the same way," he said, wishing he could take her in his arms and reassure her.

He held her hand as she got down from the truck, then made sure there was a respectable amount of space between them as they walked side by side up to the house. Even though he would like nothing more than to hold her to his side, if any of his family was watching it would be a dead giveaway that something was definitely going on between them.

"It's going to be hard as hell keeping my hands off you today," he admitted.

She laughed. "Can you imagine the look on everyone's face if you put your arm around me or kissed me?"

"That could be dangerous." He grinned. "I thought Ryder was going to have to perform the Heimlich maneuver on poor old T.J. that night in the Broken Spoke. And all I did was tell them I'd hired you to be my housekeeper."

"I can only imagine how he would react if he learned

there was more." She smiled as she reached up to press the doorbell. "Well, here we go."

"This is going to be one hell of a long day," Jaron muttered when he heard someone approaching to let them in.

When his brother Lane opened the door, he looked surprised to see Mariah with Jaron. "It's good to see both of you." He watched Lane glance at the array of parked vehicles in the driveway before his gaze swung back to Jaron. "Come on in. The guys are babysitting the kids in the game room and the women are in the kitchen."

"I'll go see if they need help finishing dinner," Mariah said, starting down the hall.

As he watched her go, Jaron couldn't keep from noticing the enticing sway of her blue-jean-clad hips. Damned if he couldn't look at that view all day long.

"Come on, bro. I've got a beer with your name on it, and you've got some explaining to do," Lane said, grinning.

Jaron followed his brother and upon entering the game room saw T.J. down on his hands and knees, giving the kids horseback rides around the pool table. The rest of his brothers were standing at the bar watching the show.

Lane walked behind the bar and uncapped a bottle of Lone Star, then handed it to Jaron. "I think our brother has something to tell us, boys."

"Is something up?" Nate Rafferty asked, perking up.

The youngest of the Raffertys, Nate and Sam were the only biological siblings of the bunch. But all six of them couldn't have been closer if they had the same blood running through their veins. Thanks to their foster father, they had bonded into a close family, and Jaron knew that every one of them would have his back when the chips were down—the same as he would have theirs.

Taking a swig of his beer, Jaron shook his head. "Nothing going on that I know of."

"Then, why did you and Mariah arrive together?" Lane asked, raising one dark eyebrow. Being a licensed psychologist, the man had a way of asking questions that cut right to the heart of the matter and in the process got the attention of everyone around him.

"You might as well tell them, Jaron," Ryder said, grinning. "You know they won't give you a minute's peace until you do."

"What do you know that we don't?" Sam asked, giving Ryder a curious glance.

Ryder shook his head. "It's Jaron's news, not mine."

"Okay, Jaron, give it up," Sam said. "What's going on with you and Mariah besides dancing around each other like two birds in a mating ritual?"

After explaining what happened three weeks ago at the Broken Spoke and what he'd learned about her losing her job and her roommate, he finished, "I needed a cook and a housekeeper and she needed a job. I offered her the position and she accepted. End of story."

"And you think having Mariah in the kitchen is going to work out?" Sam laughed. "From what Bria has told me, Mariah isn't known for her cooking abilities."

Jaron couldn't keep from grinning. "Yeah, I found

that out when she set the kitchen on fire the first morning she tried to make breakfast."

When they all stopped laughing, Nate asked, "Are you planning on losing some weight, bro?"

Jaron shook his head. "I made Mariah the ranch manager, and the first thing I had her do was to hire someone else to do the cooking and cleaning."

"But you have a degree in ranch management," Nate said, frowning. "What do you need with—" He stopped short, then, laughing out loud, got a hundred-dollar-bill out of his pocket and plunked it down on the bar. "I've got a hundred bucks that says you'll be walking down the aisle by midsummer."

"I say it'll be sooner than that," T.J. said, interrupting the kids' rides around the pool table to fish his wallet out of his hip pocket. He plunked his hundred dollars on top of Nate's. "They'll be married by the end of May."

"You're both wrong," Ryder said, looking at Jaron as if he was sizing him up. He put his money on top of the growing pile on the bar. "They'll be married by the end of next month."

"I've got this fall," Lane spoke up, adding his bet to the pot.

"I'll take Christmas," Sam said, laying his money on top of the rest.

Disgusted with his brothers, Jaron shook his head as he finished off his beer. "You're all wasting your time and money, because it's not going to happen."

Ryder tossed back the rest of his beer, then, throwing the empty bottle in the recycle bin, clapped Jaron on the shoulder. "If you'll remember, we all said the same thing when we were the ones fighting the inevitable." He laughed. "Get used to it, brother. You're one step away from joining the rest of us in the club of the blissfully hitched."

"Were you kicked in the head by a bull the last time you worked a rodeo?" Jaron asked. Before he'd retired at the ripe old age of thirty-five, Ryder had been a rodeo bullfighter and was without question the bravest man Jaron had ever known. But at the moment, he had serious questions about the man's good sense.

"Gentlemen, I hate to interrupt your lively conversation, but dinner is ready," Lane's wife, Taylor, said from the doorway.

As he and his brothers filed out of the game room and walked down the hall to take their places at the dining room table, Jaron tried to forget about their speculation and their betting pool. Nothing would make him happier than to be free to have a wife and family like they all had. But that life would never be his, and there was no sense lamenting things that he knew he'd never have.

Even if he told Mariah about his old man and she was willing to take the chance that he hadn't inherited some kind of latent cruel streak from him, Jaron wasn't. There was no way he would ever subject his wife and kid to the kind of hell he and his mother had gone through. As far as Jaron was concerned, Simon Collier's brand of crazy ended with him.

Seated at the dining room table with Bria on one side and Jaron on the other, Mariah waited until her sister was preoccupied with her son to reach beneath the tablecloth to place her hand on Jaron's thigh. Other than clearing his throat, he remained completely stoic as he covered her hand with his.

"Bria, are you feeling better?" Lane asked.

"Now that I know what the problem is, I'm feeling a lot better," her sister said, smiling. Mariah watched Bria glance at Sam before announcing, "Sam and I are going to have another baby in the fall."

"That's wonderful!" Summer McClain said from across the table. She smiled at her husband, Ryder. "We can go to doctor appointments together."

"It looks as if the family is having a baby boom," Nate said, putting his arm around his very pregnant wife, Jessie. "We're due in a month, Heather and T.J. are due this summer and both of you are due in the fall."

Mariah felt Jaron lightly squeeze her hand where it still rested on his thigh. "I'm betting you'll both have boys."

Taking her cue from him, she shook her head. "Both of them are going to have girls," she said adamantly.

She really didn't care and she knew Jaron didn't, either. They were both going to love the babies no matter what. But she knew what he was doing. They had argued about the child's gender every time one of the sisters-in-law got pregnant. The family might realize there was more going on between them than a working relationship if they didn't continue the good-natured feud.

"They're at it again," T.J. said, laughing. "How do you two work together when you can't agree on much of anything?"

"I work inside the house and he works outside the house," Mariah said, thinking quickly.

Jaron shrugged. "I've always been happier working outside."

"I can't fault you there," Ryder said, nodding. "I think if I had to be stuck inside all day I'd end up climbing the walls."

All of the men seemed to agree and Mariah relaxed when the conversation turned to talk of the calving season and plans for improvements around their ranches. By the time dinner was over and she was helping clear the table before cake and ice cream was served for Sam's birthday, she couldn't help but be a bit envious of the happy couples. They all had what she wanted—homes and families of their own.

She hoped that was in her future with Jaron. There wasn't a doubt in her mind that if he could reconcile his past it was a possibility. But what if he couldn't? What did that mean for her?

"How are things really going with you and Jaron?" Bria asked when they reached the kitchen with bowls of leftover food.

"Just fine," Mariah answered. "He works outside and I—"

"I heard you before," Bria said. "I also noticed that you two were holding hands during dinner."

"We're—" She stopped herself when she realized she really didn't know what they were. They weren't a couple and they weren't just friends.

"I don't claim to be an expert on matters of the heart," Taylor said from the other side of the kitchen island, "but ever since I became part of this family, I've seen Jaron watch you. And let me tell you, something has changed. He looks at you now as though you're the treasure at the end of the rainbow."

Setting a platter of fried chicken on the counter, Summer nodded. "That man is crazy in love with you, Mariah."

"Summer's right," Jessie said, placing containers of leftovers in the refrigerator. "He can't keep his eyes off you."

Mariah shook her head. "I know he has feelings for me, but I'm not sure I'd call it love."

"I would," Heather interjected as she dipped ice cream into dessert cups. "He looks at you the same way our husbands look at us."

Bria put her arm around Mariah. "And you've loved him since the day you met him."

"So when should we start planning your bridal shower?" Taylor asked, smiling.

Mariah shook her head. "I'm not sure it will ever come to that."

"Why not?" Bria asked.

"I'm not really sure," Mariah answered. "There's something that happened in his past that's holding him back."

"He won't talk about it because he doesn't think you'll understand?" Summer guessed.

"How did you know?" she asked, surprised.

"I had the same problem with Ryder," Summer answered.

"Even Sam waited until it almost ended our marriage before he opened up and finally told me why he got into trouble with the law when he was a teenager and how that caused him to become so driven to succeed," Bria agreed.

"I think all of them were reluctant to tell us what they'd done to get themselves sent to the Last Chance Ranch," Jessie added. "I've never seen Nate more reluctant and nervous than he was the day he told me about the trouble he got into when he was younger."

"I don't know about the others, but T.J. didn't think I'd be able to look past what he'd done years ago and accept him for who he is now," Heather said, setting the dessert cups of ice cream on a silver tray. "Silly man."

"It's a matter of trust," Summer advised. "The guys had to get used to the idea of trusting us with their greatest source of shame."

"And that isn't easy for any man," Taylor said, nodding.

"I know Jaron is a good man," Mariah insisted. "I don't care what happened when he was a boy."

"But he does, and he doesn't want you to be disappointed in him," Heather said, picking up the tray to carry it into the dining room.

"Give him time, Mariah," Bria said, giving her a hug. "When Jaron is ready, he'll take that leap of faith and tell you everything that he's trying so hard to hide because he doesn't think you'll understand."

As she and the other women walked back into the dining room, Mariah hoped they were right. Whatever secrets haunted Jaron were keeping him rooted in a very painful past, and she wanted to do whatever she could to help him move forward and leave it all behind.

Unfortunately, her fears that he might never be able to open up with her increased with each passing day. He had made progress and told her about his mother. But she had a feeling his father was the key to the worst part of his past. And until he told her what secrets he was trying to keep hidden, all she could do was love him and wait.

"You almost caused me to have a heart attack when you put your hand on my thigh during supper tonight," Jaron said when they walked into the master suite and he turned on the light.

Turning, Mariah put her arms around his neck and kissed his chin. "You looked so yummy, I couldn't help myself," she said, smiling up at the most handsome man she'd ever known.

He laughed. "Yummy, huh?"

She nodded as she pressed her lips on the pulse at the base of his throat. "All I could think about was how sexy you are and how much I wanted to kiss you and feel you touch me."

"As soon as I get these clothes off you, I intend to do both, darlin'," he said, reaching for the hem of her shirt. Leaning close, he whispered in her ear, "And I want you touching me."

"Oh, you can count on it, cowboy," she said, tugging his long-sleeve Western-cut shirt from the waistband of his jeans.

They each removed the other's clothes and in no time

at all, their clothing lay in a pile at their feet and Jaron was pulling her to him. Mariah shivered at the feel of his firm masculine flesh touching her softer feminine skin.

When he captured her lips with his, she felt as if she would melt from the heat flowing through her veins. By the time he lifted his head, her knees had failed her completely and she was sagging against him. No other man's kiss had ever affected her that way, and she knew in her heart none ever would.

The heat in his eyes caused her heart to race and her breathing to become shallow when she gazed up at him. "I—I want you now," she gasped.

He nibbled kisses down to the hollow below her ear. "But I thought you wanted me to touch you, darlin'."

Finding it hard to make her vocal cords work, she shook her head. "Please…if you don't…make love to me now…I think I'm going to…burn to a cinder."

"I want you just as much, Mariah," he said, sounding completely winded. He surprised her when he lifted her to him and in one smooth motion entered her.

Her breath caught as she wrapped her arms around his wide shoulders and her legs around his narrow hips. Resting her forehead on his shoulder, she sighed contentedly. "You feel so good…inside me."

"I intended to go…slow," he said, sounding as if he was clenching his jaw. "But I want you too damned much."

"We can go slow when we make love a little later," she said, relishing the fullness of having his body so deeply embedded in hers. "Right now, I need you to love me, Jaron."

Without another word, he carried her over to the side of the bed and sat down with her on his lap. She loved that they faced each other and would both be free to caress and kiss while their bodies moved as one.

When he began to rock them, Mariah enjoyed the friction and urgent pace of their lovemaking. Kissing his lean cheeks, the column of his neck and his collarbone, she moved in unison with him as they raced toward the culmination of the energy building inside both of them.

Feeling her feminine muscles begin to tighten around him, she clung to his shoulders to keep from being lost as she gave in to the elegant tension holding them in its grip. Apparently her release triggered his, and when he thrust into her one final time she felt him shudder as he filled her with his essence.

As they held each other while their bodies slowly drifted back to reality, she suddenly felt him go completely still. "Dammit all to hell!" he swore vehemently.

"What's wrong?" she asked, alarmed by his obvious anger.

"Mariah, I'm so sorry," he said, hugging her to him.

"Why on earth are you apologizing?" She leaned back and placed her palms on either side of his face, forced him to look at her. "What we just shared was beautiful."

He shook his head as he lifted her to sit on the bed beside him. "I was so desperate for you, I forgot to use a condom."

As the realization of what he was saying sank in, she automatically covered her lower stomach with her hand in a protective gesture. "I doubt… I mean, the odds are that I won't become pregnant," she said, trying to come to terms with the fact that she wasn't all that upset by the possibility.

What was wrong with her? The last thing she needed was an unplanned pregnancy, and especially with a man who might not ever be able to commit himself completely to their relationship.

"I've never failed to remember to use protection before," he said, rising to pace the length of the room.

"Jaron, it's not the end of the world. I'd have to do some calculations, but I don't think it's the right time of the month for that to happen," she said, trying to think if it was or not.

When he turned to make another trip across the room, she caught sight of the ugly scars marring his back for the first time. Her breath lodged in her lungs at how many of the ugly ridges crisscrossed his otherwise flawless skin.

Although she'd felt them and caught a fleeting glimpse of them a couple of times when they made love, Jaron had been careful not to let her see the extent of the damage he'd suffered. For the past week, he had already been dressed when she woke up in the mornings and she instinctively knew he'd planned it that way. But he was so angry with himself for forgetting to use protection, he had dropped his guard, and in doing so, she'd finally seen the marks he'd been trying so hard to keep hidden.

Her eyes filled with tears and, getting up from the bed, she walked over to lightly place her hand on his back. She felt him go perfectly still before he started to jerk away from her.

"Don't, Jaron," she said, catching hold of his arm to stop him.

When he turned to face her, she wrapped her arms around him and held him to her as tears streamed down her cheeks. Groaning, he pulled her closer and they simply held each other for several long minutes.

"I give you my word that I'll stand by you if you do become pregnant," he finally said, breaking the silence.

He didn't want to discuss his scars and how he got them and that was fine with her. At the moment, she couldn't think of a thing to say that wouldn't sound as though she pitied him. That was something she knew for certain that he wouldn't want to hear.

Instead, she concentrated on what he'd said about a possible pregnancy. "It never crossed my mind that you wouldn't be there for me," she said, shaking her head.

"I guess we'd better get some sleep." He released her to pick up their clothes. "I have to be up at dawn to take my shift in the calving barn."

Half an hour later as she lay in Jaron's arms, Mariah couldn't seem to turn off her thoughts. She hated to think of what he must have gone through as a child—how much emotional and physical pain he had endured. And as bad as the marks on his body were, they were nothing compared to the scars he carried that weren't visible. As long as she had a breath left in her body, she would fight like a wildcat to keep someone from doing anything like that to her child.

Her heart skipped a beat at the thought that she might

become pregnant with Jaron's baby. She'd told him that it was unlikely. But the more she thought about it, the more she realized that wasn't the case at all. She was right in the middle of her cycle, and therefore it was her most fertile time of the month.

That should have been enough to send her into a blind panic. The fact that it didn't came as a bit of a shock.

She wanted children, but did she want one now? Was she ready to become a mother?

It certainly wasn't a good time for that to happen. Knowing Jaron the way she did, if she were to become pregnant there was a very good chance he would insist that he needed to do the right thing and marry her. And as much as she loved him, that wasn't going to happen. At least, not where things stood with them now.

There were too many issues between her and Jaron that hadn't been addressed. Unfortunately, even if they did get everything out in the open, the problems might never be resolved, and bringing a child into that would be unfair to all of them. Besides, as far as she was concerned the only reason two people should consider getting married was because they loved each other and it was a natural progression of their relationship.

Forcing herself to relax, she tried to remember what Bria and the other women had told her. They had suggested that she should be patient and wait. When he was ready, he'd trust her with his secrets and tell her what had been holding him back. She could only hope they were right.

Eight

A few days after his family's get-together, Jaron propped his forearms on the top rail of one of the enclosures in the calving shed as he waited for the newborn bull calf he'd just helped deliver get to its feet. Thankfully things were slowing down with the heifers and there were only a handful left that hadn't dropped their calves. He was glad the next wave of cows to give birth had already had calves in the past and weren't as likely to have the problems a first-time mother might experience.

Every time he thought about first-time mothers or something giving birth, his heart stuttered and he had to take a deep breath in an attempt to settle himself. What if he'd made Mariah pregnant?

He still couldn't believe he'd needed her so badly that

he'd forgotten to protect her. Not one time since he'd become sexually active in his late teens had he failed to remember one of Hank's rules for life. What was there about Mariah that had caused him to lose his head and forget something as important as using a condom when they made love?

Swallowing hard, he briefly thought about having a child with her. If things were different and he'd had a halfway decent start in life, he'd like nothing more than to have a family with Mariah. But he'd never allowed himself to contemplate fatherhood, because having a kid had never been something he ever thought would happen. Unfortunately, one careless moment sure as hell had him thinking about it now.

Of course, if Mariah did become pregnant, there was no question that he'd do the right thing and make her his wife. But he couldn't help but be concerned about taking that step. Although he would gladly lay down his life to protect her and keep her from harm, how could he be sure that he hadn't inherited some part of his father's cruel nature? Even the slightest bit would be totally unacceptable.

He had no problem being able to control his temper and he'd never been prone to violent behavior. But his biggest fear had been and always would be that he'd turn out to be like his old man.

Caught up in his turbulent thoughts, Jaron welcomed the interruption when the cell phone clipped to his belt rang. But when he looked at the caller ID he felt the icy fingers of dread squeeze his chest. The call was coming from the Texas Department of Criminal Justice. He only knew one person doing time, and he was the last man on earth Jaron wanted to talk to.

How the hell had the bastard found him? When he'd had his last name changed, the judge had ordered the court records sealed due to Jaron's age and the reason for his request. And why, after twenty years with no contact between them, was his old man calling now?

Jaron's first inclination was to ignore the call. He hadn't seen or heard from his father since he'd testified against him in court all those years ago. And that was just the way he'd like to keep it. But unless Simon Collier had changed, he'd keep calling until he got hold of Jaron. That thought was even more objectionable than taking the call now.

Answering the phone, he breathed a little easier when the caller turned out to be a prison chaplain.

"Mr. Lambert, my name is Reverend John Perkins. I'm a chaplain for the Texas Department of Criminal Justice and I'm calling to let you know that your father has been transferred to the hospital unit in Galveston. I was with him when the doctor told him that he only has a few days left," the man said, his voice sympathetic. "Simon asked me to call and tell you that he wants to see you right away. There's something he needs to tell you before he passes."

"I'm sorry you wasted your time, Reverend, but he has nothing to say that I want to hear," Jaron stated flatly.

"I understand how you must feel, Mr. Lambert," the chaplain answered calmly. "Simon told me some disturbing things about his relationship with you and that he didn't treat you as well as he should have."

"That's an understatement," Jaron growled. His irritation rising, he added, "Living with Simon Collier was a living hell and I don't care to be reminded of the experience."

"I'm sure you have a lot of anger toward him, but please reconsider, son," Reverend Perkins pleaded. "This might be your last chance to see your father and make your peace with him. He asked me to stress that what he has to say is very important and something you'll want to know and need to hear."

Jaron could tell the man wasn't going to give up, and he didn't feel like explaining the many reasons he was going to ignore his old man's request. "I'm not making any promises, but I give you my word that I'll think about it," he finally conceded, hoping that would appease the man.

He would think about it, he decided. But only long enough to reject the notion outright.

"Thank you. I'll tell your father," the man said before he ended the call.

Clipping his phone back onto his belt, Jaron reached up to rub the tension tightening the back of his neck. Mariah could very well be pregnant with his baby and he had a new ranch to run. The last thing he needed piled on his already full plate was his father's dying plea to see him.

"I'm going to call it a day," he told his men. "If you need me, call the house."

"See you tomorrow, boss," one of the men called after him as he turned to leave.

When he walked out of the barn and headed toward the house, Jaron tried to forget the phone call and concentrate on spending the evening with the most exciting woman he'd ever known. As his foster father used to say, sometimes a man had to forget the past, stop thinking about the future and concentrate on the present. And that was just what he intended to do. At least for tonight.

After sharing a frozen pizza for dinner, Mariah cuddled with Jaron on the couch in the family room. He'd surprised her when he'd come in from the calving shed earlier in the afternoon and asked her to join him in the shower. That had led to them making love, and she was encouraged that he felt free enough with her to be spontaneous. But it had distracted her from something she needed to tell him, and she knew as surely as she knew her own name that the phone call she'd taken was significant and had to do with his past.

She was a little hesitant to tell him about the call. She didn't want to remind him of something that would upset him. But it might be the motivation he needed to open up and talk to her.

"When you came in this afternoon, you made me forget something I was supposed to tell you," she said, laying her head on his shoulder.

Smiling, he kissed the top of her head, then reached for the television remote. "You didn't seem to mind the distraction."

"Believe me, I'm not complaining," she said, sliding her hand inside his shirt to caress his warm skin.

"Keep that up and I'll make you forget all over again that you're supposed to tell me something," he said, giving her a promising grin.

"There was a phone call for you not long before you came in from the calving shed," she said, removing her hand from his shirt.

"Who was it?" he asked, using the remote to search for something to watch on television.

"He said his name was Reverend Perkins. He was calling from the prison hospital in Galveston." Resting against him, she noticed an immediate tensing of his muscles.

"What did he have to say?" Jaron asked, his voice tight and controlled.

"He wanted to know if he could speak to you." She sat up to look at him. "He said it was really important and—"

"Is that all he had to say?" Jaron interrupted, staring at the on-screen television guide as if it held the secrets of the universe.

"He told me...your father is dying," she said, knowing from the look on his face that the reverend telling her the nature of the call angered him.

Tossing the remote onto the coffee table, he suddenly gave up his interest in the television and rose to his feet. "He had no right to tell you that."

"I...um, asked him what the call was pertaining to," she admitted, getting up from the couch.

Turning, he pinned her with his sharp blue gaze. "Why?"

"When the man said it was important, I offered to take a message," she answered, defending herself. "That's when he told me about your dad and I immediately suggested he call your cell number."

"Don't call that bastard behind bars my dad." Jaron's voice was more of a growl than his normal baritone and the muscle working along his jawline attested to the fact that he was absolutely furious. "He may have made my mother pregnant, but he was never a father to me."

"Jaron, was he the one who caused those scars on your back?" The dark look on his face was all the answer she needed. "At some point, you're going to have to deal with your feelings about this and put it behind you or it's going to destroy you—it's going to destroy us."

"Drop it, Mariah," he warned as he started toward the foyer.

"Why won't you talk to me about it, Jaron?" she asked, following him. "Why won't you let me help you?"

"Because it's none of your concern," he said, continuing on toward the kitchen.

His sharp words cut her deeper than if he'd used a knife, but she still had to try. "Jaron, don't shut me out. Talk to me. There's nothing you could tell me that we can't get through together."

When he reached the back door, he shrugged into his jacket and grabbed his hat, crammed it on his head. "Let it alone, Mariah. There are things you don't need to know—things you don't *want* to know about me."

"Where are you going?"

"Out to the calving shed."

"Please stay and we'll work through this," she said, trying again.

"No amount of discussion is going to change a single thing, Mariah," he said, stubbornly shaking his head.

Knowing they'd reached an impasse, she warned, "Jaron, if you walk out that door, I won't be here when you get back." Her eyes filled with tears, but she blinked them away. She was determined not to let him see how badly his rejection was hurting her.

When he turned back toward her, his handsome face was devoid of all expression. He stared at her for several long moments before he reached for the doorknob. "Wait until morning. The drive over to the Sugar Creek Ranch will be safer in the daylight."

Mariah's heart felt as if it shattered into a million pieces as he walked out of the house and pulled the door shut behind him. The finality of the situation was overwhelming and tears flowed freely down her cheeks as she ran upstairs to her room.

Collapsing on the bed, she couldn't stop crying as she tried to think of what she should do. She wouldn't have given Jaron an ultimatum if she hadn't been so hurt by his telling her it was none of her business. She loved him—had always loved him—and it tore her apart that he wouldn't allow her to help him. But he had made his choice and it wasn't her.

Her heart ached more than she thought was possible as she got up and went into the closet and started throwing clothes into her overnight bag. It didn't matter that he thought she should wait until morning to leave. She wasn't about to stay where she obviously wasn't wanted.

As she grabbed her purse and overnight bag, she looked around. She'd come back to get the rest of her things in a few days after she'd had a chance to calm down.

On the drive from the Wild Maverick Ranch to Bria and Sam's, she knew that it was over for good with Jaron. Keeping his secrets from her was more important to him that she was. It was a hard realization, but one that she could no longer deny.

She had held out hope that he would one day be able to tell her about his past and she could prove to him that it didn't matter to her what he'd done all those years ago. It was the man he had become that mattered—the man she loved. But she knew now that was never going to happen.

It suddenly occurred to her that it might not be something he'd done that he was trying to hide. Given his reaction when she'd told him that the prison chaplain had called, it could very well be that it was something his father had done. But Jaron wouldn't talk to her about that, either.

When she parked the car and walked up to the Sugar Creek ranch house, Bria opened the door before Mariah had the chance to knock. Reaching out, her sister wrapped her in a comforting hug. "Are you all right?"

Shrugging, Mariah could only shake her head as a fresh wave of tears slid down her cheeks. "H-how did… you know?" she asked when the wave of emotion finally ran its course.

"Jaron called Sam to tell him that the two of you had argued and he found you gone when he returned to the house. He said he figured you were on your way over here and asked Sam to let him know you arrived safely," Bria explained. "What happened?"

"I really don't feel like going into it now," Mariah said, suddenly feeling drained of energy. "Could we talk about it tomorrow?"

"Of course," Bria said, guiding her toward the stairs.

A few minutes later, as Mariah got into bed, she curled up on her side and hugged one of the pillows to her chest in an effort to ease some of her anguish. How could everything have gone so wrong so fast? Why was he doing this to them? Why couldn't he trust that her love for him was strong enough to overlook the demons of his past and help him put them behind him for good?

Just a few short hours ago, Jaron had held her in his arms and loved her with such tenderness she'd felt as if their souls had touched. Now she was at one ranch and he was at another. And the most frustrating thing about it all was that she really didn't know why.

A couple of days after Mariah left the ranch, Jaron looked at the miserable man staring back at him in the bathroom mirror. He looked like hell and felt even worse.

He'd known up front that one day Mariah would leave, but he hadn't thought it would be this soon or that her departure would cause him to feel as though he was dying inside. All of the pain his father had inflicted on him when he was a kid was nothing compared to the debilitating ache that had settled in his chest when he'd returned to the house two nights ago and found Mariah gone.

When his cell phone rang, he glanced at the caller ID and, groaning, shook his head. He didn't want to deal with any of his well-meaning brothers right now, and especially not Lane. No amount of psychology was going to change things, and he had no doubt that Lane was going to try to draw him out and get to the bottom of what happened between him and Mariah. Ignoring the call, he let it go to voice mail and walked out of the bathroom to get dressed.

As he pulled on his clothes, he once again replayed the argument he'd had with Mariah. She'd told him that he was letting the issues with his father destroy him. Was that what he was doing by trying to hide the shame of being the son of a serial killer? It had been twenty years since he'd been the victim of his father's violent temper. By not sharing the shame of his past with Mariah, was he allowing the bastard to victimize him yet again?

Besides being sent to the Last Chance Ranch and gaining five brothers he loved and could count on to be there for him no matter what, the only other good thing that had happened in his miserable life had been Mariah. Was he going to allow the old man to destroy what he had with her?

As a kid, he'd found a way to end the abuse by turning his father in to the law. Could confronting Simon Collier now put an end to the torment for good? Or would he be dredging up things that would only make him feel worse?

The last thing Jaron wanted to do was lay eyes on the monster who had ruined his life. But if there was even the slightest chance that he could salvage what was left of his life by confronting the man, then that was exactly what he was going to do.

Six hours later, as he walked out of the prison hospital, Jaron looked up at the sky and for the first time in longer than he cared to remember, he felt as though a tremendous weight had been lifted off his shoulders. He had dreaded seeing Simon again and had damned near talked himself out of visiting the man on the drive down to Galveston. But when he walked into the room and saw the frail old man lying almost lifeless on the hospital bed, Jaron knew he'd made the right decision. It would have been cruel not to give the man his last wish and would have made Jaron no better than Simon.

But Jaron never could have imagined that one deathbed confession would set him free and give him hope of being able to build a future with the woman he loved. And, God help him, he did love Mariah.

For years he'd tried to convince himself that he was too old for her or that he wasn't the type of man she needed. He'd even gone so far as telling himself he didn't believe in love. But the truth of the matter was, from the moment he'd met Mariah, he'd been fascinated with her, and he'd used every excuse he could to be close to her. And that included arguing with her over the gender of their nieces and nephews before they were born.

He needed her as much as he needed the air he breathed, and he knew as sure as the sun rose in the east each morning that he always would. And there wasn't a doubt in his mind that she loved him just as much.

But straightening things out between them wasn't going to be easy. The other night, he had done a lot of damage to their relationship when he'd shut her out and told her his past was none of her business. She might never be able to overlook that. But if he had to get down on his hands and knees to beg her forgiveness, that was exactly what he intended to do. Nothing was more important to him than making things right with the woman who owned him heart and soul.

As he walked across the parking area to his truck and got in, he checked his watch. He had a five-hour drive to get to the Sugar Creek Ranch and a stop to make in Waco before he got there.

Swearing a blue streak, he started the truck and steered it out onto the highway headed north. Waiting until morning was one of the hardest decisions he'd ever had to make. But it would be late by the time he arrived at Sam and Bria's, and what he had to say to Mariah wasn't something that could be covered in a matter of minutes.

He released a heavy sigh as he merged into traffic on the interstate. Normally he was a very patient man. But without question he was facing the longest, most frustrating night of his life.

* * *

Sitting on the window seat in the bedroom she always used when she stayed overnight at her sister's, Mariah closed her eyes as she waited to see what the stick in her hand was going to indicate. If the claim on the back of the box was true, the test she'd chosen showed the earliest, most accurate results possible.

Unable to wait any longer, she opened one eye to peek at the tiny screen. Opening her other eye, she stared at the pregnancy test in disbelief. It not only displayed the word *pregnant*, it gave the estimated number of weeks.

"Well, that explains a lot," she murmured, placing her hand over her lower stomach.

When she'd awakened feeling sick the morning after she'd left the Wild Maverick Ranch, she'd chalked it up to having cried herself to sleep the night before. But feeling the same way two mornings in a row, she'd driven to a drugstore up in Stephenville to purchase one of the tests to rule out the possibility that she was expecting. But instead of doing that, it had confirmed that she was indeed going to have Jaron's baby.

Now what was she going to do? She was not only jobless, homeless and pregnant, she was at odds with the father of her baby.

Tears filled her eyes when she thought about the man she'd loved since she was eighteen years old. Why did he have to be so darned stubborn?

As she sat there staring at the stick in her hand, wondering how she was going to tell the love of her life that he was going to be a daddy, someone knocked on the bedroom door. "Mariah, sweetie, do you mind if I come in?" her sister asked from the other side.

Swiping at her eyes, she tucked the pregnancy test into the pocket of her jeans. "Come on in, Bria."

Her sister immediately opened the door and walked over to sit beside her on the window seat. "How are you feeling today?"

Mariah shrugged one shoulder. "About the same. Disillusioned. Hopeless. Sad. Take your pick."

Bria shook her head. "I'm not talking about your emotions. I'm asking about your morning sickness."

Shocked, Mariah turned to look at her. "How did you know?"

Smiling, Bria put her arm around Mariah's shoulders and gave her a reassuring hug. "I recognize the symptoms. When the smell of bacon frying sent you running from the kitchen yesterday morning, it raised my suspicions. When it happened again this morning, I knew for sure."

"How can you stand the smell when your cook is making breakfast?" Mariah asked. "As soon as I walked into the kitchen I thought I was going to die."

"Bacon doesn't bother me," Bria answered. "It's the smell of coffee that sends me running." She laughed. "Poor Sam has to go down to the bunkhouse now if he wants his morning coffee."

Mariah couldn't keep from feeling envious. Knowing her brother-in-law, he didn't mind at all. Sam Rafferty would walk through fire for Bria and do whatever it took to make her comfortable. She just wished Jaron felt that way about her.

"Isn't it a little soon for me to be feeling sick?" Mariah asked, glad that she had her sister to talk to about it.

Bria shook her head. "It's different for every woman and can happen at any time, although mornings are the most common. Some women get sick right away, while others don't have a problem for a few weeks. And some aren't bothered with morning sickness at all."

"You might know I wouldn't be lucky enough to be in that last group." She sighed. "Please tell me it doesn't last long."

"I wish I could," Bria said, her voice sympathetic. "It's not an exact science, and each pregnancy is different. For some women it's just a few days and others it's a couple of months. But it usually goes away by the time you get to the end of your first trimester."

Mariah groaned. "That sounds like an eternity."

Bria nodded. "It feels that way sometimes." They were silent for a few moments before she asked, "When are you going to tell Jaron?"

"I don't know." Mariah reached into her jeans pocket and withdrew the pregnancy test to show her sister. "I took this a little while ago and it indicates I'm between one and two weeks along. I guess I'll tell him when I go over to the Wild Maverick to clear out the rest of my things next week."

Bria surprised her when she laughed. "Sweetie, I don't think it will take that long."

"What do you mean?" Mariah asked, confused by her sister's speculation.

"I know Jaron loves you, and it's my guess that he won't be able to wait for you to come back to the ranch," Bria said, apparently more confident about it than Mariah was. "I think he'll be over here within the next few days. Remember how Sam came after me when we were having problems?"

"This is different," Mariah insisted. "Sam was willing to talk to you and try to work things out. Jaron refuses to do that. Knowing him, the first thing he'll do when he learns there's a baby on the way will be to tell me he'll do the right thing and we'll get married." She shook her head. "That's not going to happen. He'd want to keep his secrets even if we were married and it would end in disaster."

Bria nodded. "I can understand that. Sam's reluctance to share all of himself with me almost ended our marriage."

"I'm not sure Jaron will ever be able to open up and tell me what haunts him," Mariah said, staring down at her hands twisted into a tight knot in her lap. "One of the reasons I left the other night was because he told me that his issues were none of my business. That's not exactly the basis for a lasting relationship."

"Give him time, Mariah," Bria advised as she rose to leave. "I know he loves you. He looks at you the same way Sam looks at me."

"I know he loves me," Mariah admitted. Looking up at her sister, she shook her head. "But there are times when love just isn't enough."

Nine

The next morning, when Jaron parked his truck in Sam and Bria's driveway, he stared through the windshield at the house for several minutes before he finally took a deep breath and got out. He'd tossed and turned the entire night, going over what he intended to say to Mariah. Nothing he'd come up with was adequate to cover how bad he felt over the way he'd handled things with her.

Knocking on the back door, he waited for what seemed like forever before Sam opened it. "Hey there, Jaron. I've been expecting you. How are you doing?"

"I'm betting about the same as you when you screwed up with Bria," Jaron answered.

Sam nodded. "Yeah, I figured you've been going through hell the past few days."

"Where is she?" he asked, looking around.

"Upstairs. First door on the left." When Jaron started to cross the kitchen, Sam stopped him. "Wait a minute. I'll be right back." He disappeared into the pantry. When he returned, he shoved a box of tissues into Jaron's hands.

"What are these for?" Jaron asked, frowning.

His brother gave him a knowing smile as he rocked back on his heels. "Trust me. They'll come in handy."

Jaron groaned. "I hate when a woman cries. But when it's Mariah doing the crying, it feels as if I've been punched in the gut."

"It's our penance for screwing up," Sam agreed, nodding. "Good luck," he added when Jaron started down the hall.

When he reached the top of the stairs, he knocked on the door. He thought about calling her name, but stopped himself. For one thing, Sam and Bria's little boy might be sleeping. And for another, as bad as he'd messed up, he wasn't sure Mariah would let him in if she knew who was knocking.

"Hello, Jaron," Bria said, opening the door. She stepped back for him to enter the room. "It's good to see you."

He nodded but didn't take his eyes off Mariah sitting on the window seat across the room. She looked tired, and he figured she hadn't been sleeping any better the past few nights than he had. But it was the sadness in her eyes that just about tore him apart. He was the cause of her unhappiness and he could have kicked himself for being such a stubborn jackass.

"I'm sure the two of you have a lot to talk about,"

Bria said, stepping out into the hall. "If you need anything, I'll be downstairs with Sam."

Jaron barely noticed when his sister-in-law closed the door with a quiet click. All of his attention was focused on the beautiful woman staring at him from across the room. She looked miserable. Knowing he was the causc made him feel lower than the stuff he scraped off his boots after a trip through the barnyard.

"What do you want, Jaron?" she asked, her soft voice quieter than usual.

"I've come to take you home, where you belong," he said, crossing the distance between them to sit down beside her.

She shook her head. "The Wild Maverick is your home. Not mine."

"That's where you're wrong, darlin'," he said, shaking his head. "Without you there with me, it's just a house."

To his surprise, she got up from the window seat and turned to face him. "You made it perfectly clear the other night that I'm not *with* you. If I was, you wouldn't have told me to mind my own business."

He shook his head. "I didn't say that. I told you it wasn't your concern."

"That's just a matter of semantics, and you know it," she retorted.

She was getting angry. Good. He'd rather have her tear into him like a cougar with a sore paw than see her looking so dejected.

"You're right," he admitted, feeling about as guilty as a man possibly could. "I'm sorry, darlin'."

"You're sorry? That's all you can say?" She was gaining a full head of steam, and he didn't think he'd ever seen her look more beautiful. "You were clearly upset by that phone call about your father, which, by the way, you already knew about because Reverend Perkins called you." She looked at him accusingly. "You blamed me for the man explaining why he was trying to get in touch with you. That was unfair and we both know it."

That was exactly what he'd done, and he couldn't blame her for being furious with him. "That was wrong, and I can't tell you how much I regret reacting like that," he said honestly. "It wasn't your fault and I had no right to blame you for it."

"At least we agree on that," she said, nodding.

"Darlin', I've got some things to tell you that I think might help you understand why I acted the way I did," he said, deciding there was no easy way to explain how screwed up his life had been up to that point.

She wrapped her arms around herself protectively and he hated that she felt so wary with him. Unfortunately, her caution was no less than he deserved. He'd been a complete ass about the matter.

"Please sit down and listen to what I have to say, Mariah," he requested.

After years of trying to keep his past concealed, revealing what he'd gone through wasn't going to be easy for him. But there were things she needed to know if there was any chance of them having a future together.

Instead of sitting beside him on the window seat, she lowered herself to the side of the bed, facing him. "Okay, I'm listening."

He took a deep breath. "You were right about my father causing the scars on my back. He had a violent temper and I was a convenient outlet for his anger." He shrugged. "It didn't matter if I had done something or not—I was there and too young to fight back."

"I'm so sorry," she said, her eyes filled with sympathy. "No child deserves that kind of treatment."

He shook his head. "I'm not telling you any of this because I want you to feel sorry for me. I want you to understand why I've spent my life trying to hide it."

"Continue," she said, nodding.

"I think I told you I lost my mom."

She nodded. "You said you were six when she died and that you didn't know what happened."

"What I said was one day she was gone and I knew I'd never see her again. I never said I didn't know what happened to her." He stared down at the toes of his boots for a moment before he looked up to see Mariah watching him. "My mom didn't die of natural causes. The bastard she was married to killed her."

"Oh, my God," she gasped, covering her mouth with her hand. "Did you witness the murder?"

Shaking his head, he explained, "Her body was never found because nobody knew to look for her. He told everyone, including me, that she took off. I didn't find out what happened to her until I was thirteen. He got pissed off about something, and while he was taking out his anger on me, he let it slip that he should kill me and do away with my body the same way he had done with my mother."

Mariah's eyes widened in horror and he hated having to share the ugliness of his life with her. But they couldn't move forward until she knew it all.

"I knew that it was only a matter of time before he carried through on it and I disappeared the way my mom did." He reached up to rub the tension building at the back of his neck. "I was the one who turned him in to the police."

"That's why he's in prison, isn't it?" she asked as tears filled her eyes. "Because he killed your mother."

"Yes and no," he admitted, opening the box of tissues Sam had given him.

She looked confused as she accepted the tissue he handed her. "You want to explain that?"

He released a heavy sigh. "At first, the cops thought I was just a kid with a grudge against my father. After I showed them the scars on my back, they picked him up for child abuse." He shook his head. "I kept trying to tell them about my mom, but they focused on the abuse that I had suffered instead of what had happened to her. When they arrested him and brought him in to police headquarters, he saw me and all hell broke loose."

"What did he do?" Unable to bear the horrified expression on her pretty face, Jaron trained his gaze on a picture of her and Bria when they were little girls hanging on the wall across the room.

"He went into a tirade and without thinking repeated his regrets that he hadn't killed me the way he'd done my mom." Jaron shook his head. "During the investigations, they weren't able to find any evidence that he killed her, but they found enough to tie him to a few other murders and suspect him of several more. Along with the charges of child abuse, they had enough to put him away for life."

"Dear God, he..."

When her voice trailed off, Jaron finished for her. "He was a serial killer."

To his relief, instead of Mariah looking at him with suspicion the way some people had, tears streamed down her cheeks when she got up from the bed and came over to sit down beside him on the window seat, then put her arms around him. "I hate that you had to go through all that, Jaron."

He wrapped his arms around her, and for the first time in three days felt the sense of contentment that he only experienced with Mariah. "Don't cry, darlin'. I survived."

"But why were you so reluctant to tell me about all of this?" she asked.

"When Simon was arrested, I was put into foster care," he explained. "You'd be amazed at the number of foster families who refuse to take in the kid of a serial killer. And the ones who did open their homes to me acted as if they thought I might be a danger to them."

She looked puzzled. "Why would they do that?"

"I guess they were afraid that I would turn out to have tendencies like the old man," Jaron said, shrugging.

"That's why you wanted to keep everything about your past hidden, isn't it?" she guessed. "You didn't trust that I wouldn't do the same thing."

He nodded. "It wasn't until I was sent to the Last

Chance Ranch that I felt accepted for who I was—just a kid caught up in a bad situation."

"But I thought only boys who were in trouble with the law were sent to live with Hank Calvert," she said, frowning.

He smiled. "I had a bad habit of running away from foster homes when I got tired of them looking at me as though they were afraid I'd kill them in their sleep."

"That was unfair," she said indignantly. "You had nothing to do with your father's crimes."

"Unfair or not, I learned that if I wanted to be treated like everyone else, I kept my mouth shut and didn't let anyone know whose kid I was." Unable to stop himself, he kissed her forehead. "I was afraid if you knew what had happened, you might look at me that way, too." He shook his head. "I couldn't stand the thought of that."

"I suppose I can understand how you felt. But I've known all along that your past was sketchy and I didn't care," she reminded him.

He nodded. "I guess I was just so conditioned to having people look at me differently once they found out who I was, I expected everyone would. Hell, I even started to fear that one day my father's cruel streak could show up in me."

"That's ridiculous," Mariah said, defending him. "There isn't a cruel bone in your body."

"Thank you for believing in me, darlin'." He swallowed around the sudden lump clogging his throat. "But the way I talked to you the other night, I don't deserve it."

"You were upset," she said, shrugging one shoulder.

He shook his head. "That's no excuse for treating you that way."

They fell silent for a few minutes before she asked, "Did you go see your father?"

"I went to see Simon Collier."

"Who's that?" Mariah asked, looking confused.

"My stepfather," Jaron said, still getting used to the fact that the man wasn't his real father. "The reason he insisted that he had to see me before he died was because he wanted to clear his conscience. He asked my forgiveness for the beatings, then told me that my mother was already pregnant when he married her and he wasn't my biological father."

"But if you didn't know that, why didn't you question your last name being different than his?" she asked, frowning.

He smiled. "Due to the nature of his crimes and the reluctance of foster families taking me in, my caseworker talked to the judge and I was allowed to change my surname to my mother's maiden name."

"I'm happy he did the right thing and told you he wasn't your father," she stated.

"I am, too." Jaron smiled. "I know now that I didn't inherit his mean streak and can't pass that on to the next generation." He picked her up and set her on his lap. "Now that you know all about me, I have something I've been wanting to ask you."

"Okay," she said cautiously. "What is it?"

"Why am I the one you chose to take your virginity?" he asked.

"Why do you think?" she asked evasively.

"I hope it's because you love me," he said, knowing that was exactly why she'd made love with him.

"I'm not saying that's the reason, but how would you feel if that was the case?" she asked, looking cautious.

"I'd be the happiest man alive," he admitted, smiling. "It makes it a whole lot easier knowing that the woman I love more than life itself loves me back."

Fresh tears filled her emerald eyes. "You love me?"

"Mariah, I've loved you since the moment we met," he said honestly. "I just didn't want to saddle you with the baggage that came along with me."

"Oh, Jaron, I've wanted to hear you say that for so long," she admitted. "I love you more than you'll ever know."

"And I love you just as much," he said, kissing her soft lips. That seemed to open the floodgates, and he hoped the tears she now shed were happy ones.

When her crying ran its course, he handed her more tissues, and while she wiped away the last traces of her tears, he pulled a small black velvet box from his jeans pocket. He'd stopped at an exclusive jewelry store in Waco on his way back from the prison hospital, and he hoped she liked the ring he'd chosen.

Setting her on the window seat, he got down on one knee in front of her and opened the box with a two-carat marquis diamond inside. "Darlin', I know I'm not nearly good enough for you, but I love you and I promise I'll spend the rest of my days doing everything I can to make you happy. Will you marry me?"

"Only on one condition," she said, her eyes filled with more love than he would ever deserve.

"What's that, darlin'?" he asked, knowing he would agree to anything as long as she agreed to share her life with him.

"No more secrets," she stated. "I want nothing but complete honesty between us."

He nodded. "Mariah, I give you my word that I will never hold anything back with you ever again." Removing the ring from the box he held, he asked, "Now will you make me the happiest man alive and tell me you'll be my wife?"

"Y-yes!" she said, throwing her arms around his neck.

When he slipped the ring on her finger, it seemed to induce another wave of tears, and Jaron was glad his brother had the foresight to send the box of tissues upstairs with him. Scooping her up, he sat back down on the window seat with her on his lap and held her while she cried against his chest.

"I—I have…something…I need to tell you," she said, sniffing back more tears.

"I'm all ears, darlin'," he said, feeling happier than he'd ever felt in his entire life. "You can tell me anything."

"I took a pregnancy test this morning," she said, causing him to catch his breath.

"And?"

Reaching into her pocket, she handed him a white plastic stick with purple trim on it. The message on the tiny screen had his heart pumping double-time.

Completely dumbfounded, he couldn't have strung words together if his life depended on it.

"We're going to have a baby," Mariah said, looking as if she was unsure how he would take the news.

"I love you, Mariah, and I couldn't be happier." Kissing her until they both gasped for breath, he grinned. "In the past few minutes, you've given me everything I never thought I would have."

They held each other for some time before she asked, "When do you want to get married?"

"Is this afternoon too soon?" he teased.

"That would be nice, but there's a waiting period, and I doubt they would waive that just because you're impatient," she said, laughing.

"I'm good with whatever you want, darlin'," he said, meaning it. "You plan it and I'll see that it happens."

"Why don't we go home, and after you make love to me, we'll start planning our wedding?" she whispered in his ear.

It felt as though molten lava flowed through his veins at her suggestion. "I like the way you think."

She gave him a smile that lit the darkest corners of his soul. "Then, take me home, cowboy."

Two weeks later, as Jaron stood in front of the fireplace in Sam and Bria's living room, he checked his watch. His sisters-in-law had insisted that it was bad luck for the groom to see the bride before the wedding and Mariah had spent the night upstairs in the room where he'd proposed. It seemed like an eternity since he'd held her, and he vowed right then and there that for as long as he lived, he'd never spend another night away from her.

"Getting cold feet, bro?" Nate asked as they faced the rest of the family.

"Not at all." Jaron grinned. "I'm just looking forward to getting the honeymoon started."

His brother nodded. "I felt the same way when Jessie and I got married. Did you ever think when we were raising hell out on the rodeo circuit that we'd be happy settling down with one woman and having a bunch of little kids?"

"No, I can't say that I did," Jaron answered.

When the beginning notes of "Here Comes the Bride" came from the house audio system, Jaron fixed his gaze on the door that led out into the foyer and waited for Sam to escort the woman of his dreams across the room to join him in front of the pastor. In just a few short minutes, he and Mariah would be husband and wife, and as far as he was concerned it couldn't happen soon enough.

As Bria walked through the doorway and across the room to stand on the other side of the fireplace, he barely noticed. His eyes were trained on Mariah in her long white wedding gown as Sam walked her toward him. She looked absolutely gorgeous, and he swallowed hard at the thought that a woman so beautiful would fall in love with a dust-covered cowboy like himself.

"Are you ready for this?" he asked, taking her hand from Sam.

"I've been waiting all my life for you," she said, smiling.

"And I've been waiting just as long for you," he said, kissing her cheek. "Let's make this official."

* * *

An hour later, as Jaron stood at the bar with his brothers having a drink to toast his and Mariah's marriage, his gaze kept drifting to his new wife. She owned him heart, body and soul, and he couldn't have been happier about it.

"Well, now that I've won the pool for when Jaron and Mariah would get married and we've all joined the club of the blissfully hitched, what are we going to bet on next?" Ryder asked.

"How many kids we're all going to have?" T.J. asked, grinning.

Lane shook his head. "We wouldn't know the outcome of that for years."

"Mariah and I were talking the other day about the Last Chance Ranch and what a difference it made in all of our lives," Jaron said, watching her and the other women laughing at something one of the kids had done. "What do you think about giving other kids the same chance we had?"

"You've got my attention," Sam spoke up.

Lane nodded. "What do you have in mind?"

"I think we should buy some land and build the Hank Calvert Memorial Last Chance Ranch," Jaron answered.

"We've got a board of directors right here," T.J. said, nodding.

"And it's not as though we don't have our own psychologist to oversee the programs the kids would need," Ryder added.

"I think Hank would approve wholeheartedly," Sam said, looking thoughtful.

"If there's a chance of giving kids the lives that Hank gave us, I say go for it," Nate agreed.

"Then, it's settled," Jaron said decisively. "We can get things set up and look for a piece of land as soon as Mariah and I get back from our honeymoon. Why don't we bet on how long it's going to take to get the ranch up and running?"

"Sounds good to me," his brothers said almost in unison.

"We'll start the betting pool and get things set up as soon as you get back from your honeymoon," Ryder said.

Jaron grinned as he set his beer bottle on the bar. "If my wife is ready, we'll go get started on *that* right now."

Walking over to Mariah, he took her in his arms. "Are you ready to leave, Mrs. Lambert?"

"I thought you'd never ask," she said, kissing his chin.

Saying their goodbyes, they walked hand in hand out to their newly purchased minivan. "I'm glad we decided on Hawaii for our honeymoon," Mariah said as he helped her into the passenger seat. "It may be the last time I get to wear a bikini for a while."

"Why do you say that, darlin'?"

"I'm going to be having lots of little Lamberts in the next several years," she said.

Staring at the woman he loved with all his heart, he grinned. "I'll be more than happy to help you with that, darlin'."

"I love you, cowboy," she said, giving him a smile that sent his blood pressure soaring.

"And I love you, darlin'. Forever and always."

Epilogue

One year later

As Jaron looked around the reception hall following the ground-breaking ceremony for the Hank Calvert Memorial Last Chance Ranch, he smiled. The turn-out couldn't have been better. Several politicians had shown up, as well as the head of the Texas foster-care system and most of her staff. There were also quite a few members of the media covering the event. Jaron wasn't surprised. Hank had been well-respected for the difference he'd made in the lives of the kids most people had given up on as lost causes. Jaron hoped that the ranch he and his brothers were setting up for troubled youth carried on Hank's legacy.

"It looks as though the ranch is well on its way to

becoming a reality," Sam said, checking the bottle he was giving to his new baby son.

Jaron nodded. "I think Hank would approve."

"I know he would," Lane said, setting his little boy on his feet to run over to his mother. "Hank would be proud to know the boys he saved from a life behind bars or an early grave were going to give other troubled kids the same chance he gave us."

Nate patted his sleeping daughter's back when she raised her head a moment before falling back to sleep. "Hank always told us to do something about it whenever we saw a need," he added quietly to keep from disturbing the baby.

They all nodded a moment before Ryder's groan drew their attention. "The smell of a clean shirt nauseates this baby the same as it did her big sister."

"I think that's true for all babies," T.J. said, joining them. He was wearing a different shirt than the one he'd worn for the ground breaking. "Heather always puts an extra shirt in the diaper bag for me the same as she does for the boys."

"Try keeping your shirt clean with twins," Jaron said, laughing. "It's just not going to happen."

Nate grinned. "Since you always insisted that our babies would be boys and Mariah argued that they would be girls, it's only fitting that you ended up with one of each."

"Our family sure has grown a lot in the past few years," T.J. said, looking around the reception hall.

"No kidding," Sam agreed. "Between the six of us, we have ten kids."

"And they're all under the age of four," Lane added.

Ryder laughed. "Who would have ever thought four years ago that we'd be standing around talking about babies instead of the merits of a Brahman cross over a purebred bucking bull?"

"Jaron, could you watch Alisa while I change Brett?" Mariah asked, pushing the stroller up beside him.

"No problem." He waited until she picked up their smiling son, then kissed her cheek and whispered in her ear, "Thank you, darlin'."

"For what?" she asked, smiling back at him.

"You didn't give up on me when you had every reason to," he said, meaning it. "You and the kids are my world and I never want you to doubt how much I love all of you."

"And we love you, cowboy." The deep emotion he detected in her emerald eyes robbed him of breath.

"How would you like to head home and get the kids down for a nap as soon as you change our son's diaper?" he asked, needing to show her how much he cherished her. "I'd really like to make love to their mother."

"I like the way you think, cowboy." She gave him a smile that sent his hormones into overdrive. "Let's hope we can stay awake long enough for that."

He laughed. "Yeah, that's something we haven't had a whole lot of lately."

"We probably can't count on much of that for another eighteen years or so," Mariah said, grinning as she headed toward the ladies' room to change their baby boy.

As he watched her disappear down the hall, Jaron

couldn't help but feel blessed. He had the love of a good woman, two beautiful babies and a band of brothers who had his back no matter what. And all because as a troubled kid he'd been lucky enough to be sent to the Last Chance Ranch.

* * * * *

NEVER TOO LATE

Brenda Jackson

Chapter 1

Twelve days and counting...

Pushing a lock of twisted hair that had fallen in her face behind her ear, Sienna Bradford, soon to become Sienna Davis once again, straightened her shoulders as she walked into the cabin she'd once shared with her husband—soon-to-be ex-husband.

She glanced around. Had it been just three years ago when Dane had brought her here for the first time? Three years ago when the two of them had sat there in front of the fireplace after making love, and planned their wedding? Promising that no matter what, their marriage would last forever? She took a deep breath knowing that for them, forever would end in twelve days in Judge Ratcliff's chambers.

Just thinking about it made her heart ache, but she

decided it wouldn't help matters to have a pity party. What was done was done and things just hadn't worked out between her and Dane like they'd hoped. There was nothing to do now but move on with her life. But first, according to a letter her attorney had received from Dane's attorney a few days ago, she had ten days to clear out any and all of her belongings from the cabin, and the sooner she got the task done, the better. Dane had agreed to let her keep the condo if she returned full ownership of the cabin to him. She'd had no problem with that, since he had owned it before they married.

Sienna crossed the room, shaking off the March chill. According to forecasters, a snowstorm was headed toward the Smoky Mountains within the next seventy-two hours, which meant she had to hurry and pack up her stuff and take the two-hour drive back to Charlotte. Once she got home she intended to stay inside and curl up in bed with a good book. Sienna smiled, thinking that a "do nothing" weekend was just what she needed in her too frantic life.

Her smile faded when she considered that since starting her own interior decorating business a year and a half ago, she'd been extremely busy—and she had to admit that was when her marital problems with Dane had begun.

Sienna took a couple of steps toward the bedroom to begin packing her belongings when she heard the sound of the door opening. Turning quickly, she suddenly remembered she had forgotten to lock the door. Not smart when she was alone in a secluded cabin high up in the mountains, and a long way from civilization.

A scream quickly died in her throat when the person who walked in—standing a little over six feet with dark eyes, close-cropped black hair, chestnut coloring and a medium build—was none other than her soon-to-be ex.

From the glare on his face, she could tell he wasn't happy to see her. But so what? She wasn't happy to see him, either, and couldn't help wondering why he was there.

Before she could swallow the lump in her throat to ask, he crossed his arms over his broad chest, intensified his glare and said in that too sexy voice she knew so well, "I thought that was your car parked outside, Sienna. What are you doing here?"

Chapter 2

Dane wet his suddenly dry lips and immediately decided he needed a beer. Lucky for him there was a six-pack in the refrigerator from the last time he'd come to the cabin. But he didn't intend on moving an inch until Sienna told him what she was doing there.

She was nervous, he could tell. Well, that was too friggin bad. She was the one who'd filed for the divorce—he hadn't. But since she had made it clear that she wanted him out of her life, he had no problem giving her what she wanted, even if the pain was practically killing him. But she'd never know that.

"What do you think I'm doing here?" she asked smartly, reclaiming his absolute attention.

"If I knew, I wouldn't have asked," he said, giving her the same unblinking stare. And to think that at one time he actually thought she was his whole world. At some point during their marriage she had changed and transitioned into quite a character—someone he was certain he didn't know anymore.

She met his gaze for a long, level moment before placing her hands on her hips. Doing so drew his attention to her body; a body he'd seen naked countless times, a body he knew as well as his own; a body he used to ease into during the heat of passion to receive pleasure so keen and satisfying, just thinking about it made him hard.

"The reason I'm here, Dane Bradford, is because your attorney sent mine this nasty little letter demanding that I remove my stuff within ten days, and this weekend was better than next weekend. However, no thanks to you, I still had to close the shop early to beat traffic and the bad weather."

He actually smiled at the thought of her having to do that. "And I bet it almost killed you to close your shop early. Heaven forbid. You probably had to cancel a couple of appointments. Something I could never get you to do for me."

Sienna rolled her eyes. They'd had this same argument over and over again and it all boiled down to the same thing. He thought her job meant more to her than he did because of all the time she'd put into it. But what really irked her with that accusation was that before she'd even entertained the idea of quitting her job and embarking on her own business, they had talked about it and what it would mean. She would have to work her butt off and network to build a new clientele; and then there would be time spent working on decorating proposals, spending long hours in many beautiful homes of the rich and famous. And he had understood and had been supportive…at least in the beginning.

But then he began complaining that she was spending too much time away from home, away from him. Things only got worse from there, and now she was a woman who had gotten married at twenty-four and was getting divorced at twenty-seven.

"Look, Dane, it's too late to look back, reflect and complain. In twelve days you'll be free of me and I'll be free of you. I'm sure there's a woman out there who has the time and patience to—"

"Now, that's a word you don't know the meaning of, Sienna," Dane interrupted. "*Patience.* You were always in a rush, and your tolerance level for the least little thing was zero. Yeah, I know I probably annoyed the hell out of you at times. But then there were times you annoyed me, as well. Neither of us is perfect."

Sienna let out a deep breath. "I never said I was perfect, Dane."

"No, but you sure as hell acted like you thought you were, didn't you?"

Chapter 3

Dane's question struck a nerve. Considering her background, how could he assume Sienna thought she was perfect? She had come from a dysfunctional family if ever there was one. Her mother hadn't loved her father, her father loved all women except her mother, and neither seemed to love their only child. Sienna had always combated lack of love with doing the right thing, thinking that if she did, her parents would eventually love her. It didn't work. But still, she had gone through high school and college being the good girl, thinking being good would eventually pay off and earn her the love she'd always craved.

In her mind, it had when she'd met Dane, the man least likely to fall in love with her. He was the son of the millionaire Bradfords who'd made money in land development. She hadn't been his family's choice and they made sure she knew it every chance they got. Whenever she was around them, they made her feel inadequate, like she didn't measure up to their society friends, and since she didn't come from a family with a prestigious background, she wasn't good enough for their son.

She bet they wished they'd never hired the company she'd been working for to decorate their home. That's how she and Dane had met. She'd been going over fabric swatches with his mother and he'd walked in after playing a game of tennis. The rest was history. But the question of the hour was: Had she been so busy trying to succeed the past year and a half, trying to be the perfect business owner, that she eventually alienated the one person who'd mattered most to her?

"Can't answer that. Can you?" Dane said, breaking into her thoughts. "Maybe that will give you something to think about twelve days from now when you put your John Hancock on the divorce papers. Now if you'll excuse me, I have something to do," he said, walking around her toward the bedroom.

"Wait. You never said why *you're* here!"

He stopped. The intensity of his gaze sent shivers of heat through her entire body. And it didn't help matters that he was wearing jeans and a dark brown leather bomber jacket that made him look sexy as hell… as usual. "I was here a couple of weekends ago and left something behind. I came to get it."

"Were you alone?" The words rushed out before she could hold them back and immediately she wanted to smack herself. The last thing she wanted was for him to think she cared…even if she did.

He hooked his thumbs in his jeans and continued to hold her gaze. "Would it matter to you if I weren't?"

She couldn't look at him, certain he would see her lie when she replied, "No, it wouldn't matter. What you do is none of my business."

"That's what I thought." And then he walked off toward the bedroom and closed the door.

Sienna frowned. That was another thing she didn't like about Dane. He never stayed around to finish one of their arguments. Thanks to her parents she was a pro at it, but Dane would always walk away after giving some smart parting remark that only made her that much more angry. He didn't know how to fight fair. He didn't know how to fight at all. He'd come from a family too dignified for such nonsense.

Moving toward the kitchen to see if there was anything of hers in there, Sienna happened to glance out the window.

"Oh, my God," she said, rushing over to the window. It was snowing already. No, it wasn't just snowing… There was a full-scale blizzard going on outside. What happened to the seventy-two-hour warning?

She heard Dane when he came out of the bedroom. He looked beyond her and out the window, uttering one hell of a curse word before quickly walking to the door, slinging it open and stepping outside.

In just that short period of time, everything was beginning to turn white. The last time they'd had a sudden snowstorm such as this had been a few years ago. It had been so bad the media had nicknamed it the “Beast from the East.”

It seemed the Beast was back and it had turned downright spiteful. Not only was it acting ugly outside, it had placed Sienna in one hell of a predicament. She was stranded in a cabin in the Smoky Mountains with her soon-to-be ex. Things couldn’t get any more bizarre than that.

Chapter 4

Moments later, when Dane stepped back into the cabin, slamming the door behind him, Sienna could tell he was so mad he could barely breathe.

"What's wrong, Dane? You being forced to cancel a date tonight?" she asked snidely. A part of her was still upset at the thought that he might have brought someone here a couple of weekends ago when they weren't officially divorced yet. The mere fact they had been separated for six months didn't count. She hadn't gone out with anyone. Indulging in a relationship with another man hadn't even crossed her mind.

He took a step toward her and she refused to back up. She was determined to maintain her ground and her composure, although the intense look in his eyes was causing crazy things to happen to her body, like it normally did whenever they were alone for any period of time. There may have been a number of things wrong with their marriage, but lack of sexual chemistry had never been one of them.

"Do you know what this means?" he asked, his voice shaking in anger.

She tilted her head to one side. "Other than I'm being forced to remain here with you for a couple of hours, no, I don't know what it means."

She saw his hands ball into fists at his sides and knew he was probably fighting the urge to strangle her. "We're not talking about hours, Sienna. Try days. Haven't you been listening to the weather reports?"

She glared at him. "Haven't you? I'm not here by myself."

"Yes, but I thought I could come up here and in ten minutes max get what I came for, and leave before the bad weather kicked in."

Sienna regretted that she hadn't been listening to the weather reports, at least not in detail. She'd known that a snowstorm was headed toward the mountains within seventy-two hours, which was why she'd thought, like Dane, that she had time to rush and get in and out before the nasty weather hit. Anything other than that, she was clueless. And what was he saying about them being up here for days instead of hours? "Yes, I did listen to the weather reports, but evidently I missed something."

He shook his head. "Evidently you missed a lot, if you think this storm is going to blow over in a couple of hours. According to forecasters, what you see isn't the worst of it, and because of that unusual cold front hovering about in the east, it may last for days."

She swallowed deeply. The thought of spending *days* alone in a cabin with Dane didn't sit well with her. "How many days are we talking about?"

"Try three or four."

She didn't want to try any at all, and as she continued to gaze into his eyes she saw a look of worry replace the anger in their dark depths. Then she knew what had him upset.

"Do we have enough food and supplies up here to hold us for three or four days?" she asked, as she began to nervously gnaw on her lower lip. The magnitude of the situation they were in was slowly dawning on her, and when he didn't answer immediately she knew they were in trouble.

Chapter 5

Dane saw the panic that suddenly lined Sienna's face. He wished he could say he didn't give a damn, but there was no way that he could. This woman would always matter to him whether she was married to him or not. From the moment he had walked into his father's study that day and their gazes had connected, he had known then, as miraculous at it had seemed, and without a word spoken between them, that he was meant to love her. And for a while he had convinced her of that, but not anymore. Evidently, at some point during their marriage, she began believing otherwise.

"Dane?"

He rubbed his hand down his face, trying to get his thoughts together. Given the situation they were in, he knew honesty was foremost. But then he'd always been honest with her, however, he doubted she could say the same for herself. "To answer your question, Sienna, I'm not sure. Usually I keep the place well stocked of everything, but like I said earlier, I was here a couple of weekends ago, and I used a lot of the supplies then."

He refused to tell her that in a way it had been her fault. Receiving those divorce papers had driven him here, to wallow in self-pity, vent out his anger and drink his pain away with a bottle of Johnny Walker Red. "I guess we need to go check things out," he said, trying not to get as worried as she was beginning to look.

He followed her into the kitchen, trying not to watch the sway of her hips as she walked in front of him. The hot, familiar sight of her in a pair of jeans and pullover sweater had him cursing under his breath and summoning up a quick remedy for the situation he found himself in. The thought of being stranded for any amount of time with Sienna wasn't good.

He stopped walking when she flung open the refrigerator. His six-pack of beer was still there, but little else. But then he wasn't studying the contents of the refrigerator as much as he was studying her. She was bent over, looking inside, but all he could think of was another time he had walked into this kitchen and found her in that same position, and wearing nothing more than his T-shirt that had barely covered her bottom. It hadn't taken much for him to go into a crazed fit of lust and quickly remove his pajama bottoms and take her right then and there, against the refrigerator, giving them both the orgasm of a lifetime.

"Thank goodness there are some eggs in here," she

said, intruding on his heated thoughts down memory lane. "About half a dozen. And there's a loaf of bread that looks edible. There's some kind of meat in the freezer, but I'm not sure what it is, though. Looks like chicken."

She turned around and her pouty mouth tempted him to kiss it, devour it and make her moan. He watched her sigh deeply and then she gave him a not-so-hopeful gaze and said, "Our rations don't look good, Dane. What are we going to do?"

Chapter 6

Sienna's breath caught when the corners of Dane's mouth tilted in an irresistible smile. She'd seen the look before. She knew that smile and she also recognized that bulge pressing against his zipper. She frowned. "Don't even think it, Dane."

He leaned back against the kitchen counter. Hell, he wanted to do more than think it, he wanted to do it. But, of course, he would pretend he hadn't a clue as to what she was talking about. "What?"

Her frown deepened. "And don't act all innocent with me. I know what you were thinking."

A smile tugged deeper at Dane's lips knowing she probably did. There were some things a man couldn't hide and a rock-solid hard-on was one of them. He decided not to waste his time and hers pretending the chemistry between them was dead when they both knew it was still very much alive. "Don't ask me to apologize. It's not my fault you have so much sex appeal and my desire for you is automatic, even when we're headed for divorce court."

Dane saying the word *divorce* was a stark reminder that their life together, as they once knew it, would be over in twelve days. "Let's get back to important matters, Dane, like our survival. On a positive note, we might be able to make due if we cut back on meals, which may be hard for you with your ferocious appetite."

A wicked sounding chuckle poured from his throat. "Which one?"

Sienna swallowed as her pulse pounded in response to Dane's question. She was quickly reminded, although she wished there was some way she could forget, that her husband…or soon-to-be ex…did have two appetites. One was of a gastric nature and the other purely sexual. Thoughts of the purely sexual one had intense heat radiating all through her. Dane had devoured every inch of her body in ways she didn't even want to think about. Especially now.

She placed her hands on her hips knowing he was baiting her; really doing a hell of a lot more than that. He was stirring up feelings inside her that were making it hard for her to think straight. "Get serious, Dane."

"I am." He then came to stand in front of her. "Did you bring anything with you?"

She lifted a brow. "Anything like what?"

"Stuff to snack on. You're good for that. How you do it without gaining a pound is beyond me."

She shrugged, refusing to tell him that she used to work it off with all those in-bed, out-of-bed exercises they used to do. If he hadn't noticed then she wouldn't tell him that in six months without him in her bed, she had gained five pounds. "I might have a candy bar or two in the car."

He smiled. "That's all?"

She rolled her eyes upward. "Okay, okay, I might have a couple of bags of chips, too." She decided not to mention the three boxes of Girl Scout cookies that had been purchased that morning from a little girl standing in front of a grocery store.

"I hadn't planned to spend the night here, Dane. I had merely thought I could quickly pack things and leave."

He nodded. "Okay, I'll get the snacks from your car while I'm outside checking on some wood we'll need for the fire. The power is still on, but I can't see that lasting too much longer. I wished I would have gotten that generator fixed."

Her eyes widened in alarm. "You didn't?"

"No. So you might want to go around and gather up all the candles you can. And there should be a box of matches in one of these drawers."

"Okay."

Dane turned to leave. He then turned back around. She was nibbling on her bottom lip as he assumed she would be. "And stop worrying. We're going to make it."

When he walked out the room, Sienna leaned back against the closed refrigerator, thinking those were the exact words he'd said to her three years ago when he had asked her to marry him. Now she *was* worried because they didn't have a proved track record.

Chapter 7

After putting on the snow boots he kept at the cabin, Dane made his way out the doors, grateful for the time he wouldn't be in Sienna's presence. Being around her and still loving her like he did was hard. Even now he didn't know the reason for the divorce, other than what was noted in the papers he'd been served that day a few weeks ago. Irreconcilable differences…whatever the hell that was supposed to mean.

Sienna hadn't come to him so they could talk about any problems they were having. He had come home one day and she had moved out. He still was at a loss as to what could have been so wrong with their marriage that she could no longer see a future for them.

He would always recall that time as being the lowest point in his life. For days it was as if a part of him was missing. It had taken a while to finally pull himself together and realize she wasn't coming back no matter how many times he'd asked her to. And all it took was the receipt of that divorce petition to make him realize that Sienna wanted him out of her life, and actually believed that whatever issues kept them apart couldn't be resolved.

A little while later Dane had gathered more wood to put with the huge stack already on the back porch, glad that at least, if nothing else, they wouldn't freeze to death. The cabin was equipped with enough toiletries to hold them for at least a week, which was a good thing. And he hadn't wanted to break the news to Sienna that the meat in the freezer wasn't chicken, but deer meat that one of his clients had given him a couple of weeks ago after a hunting trip. It was good to eat, but he knew Sienna well enough to know she would have to be starving before she would consume any of it.

After rubbing his icy hands on his jeans, he stuck them into his pockets to keep them from freezing. Walking around the house, he strolled over to her car, opened the door and found the candy bars, chips and… Girl Scout cookies, he noted, lifting a brow. She hadn't mentioned them, and he saw they were her favorite kind, as well as his. He quickly recalled the first year they were married and how they shared the cookies as a midnight snack after making love. He couldn't help but smile as he remembered that night and others where they had spent time together, not just in bed but cooking in the kitchen, going to movies, concerts, parties, having picnics and just plain sitting around and talking for hours.

He suddenly realized that one of the things that had been missing from their marriage for a while was communication. When had they stopped talking? The first thought that grudgingly came to mind was when she'd begun bringing work home, letting it intrude on what had always been their time together. That's when they had begun living in separate worlds.

Dane breathed in deeply. He wanted to get back into Sienna's world and he definitely wanted her back in his. He didn't want a divorce. He wanted to keep his wife but he refused to resort to any type of manipulating, dominating or controlling tactics to do it. What he and Sienna needed was to use this weekend to keep it honest and talk openly about what had gone wrong with their marriage. They would go further by finding ways to resolve things. He still loved her and wanted to believe that deep down she still loved him.

There was only one way to find out.

Chapter 8

Sienna glanced around the room seeing all the lit candles and thinking just how romantic they made the cabin look. Taking a deep breath, she frowned in irritation, thinking that romance should be the last thing on her mind. Dane was her soon-to-be ex-husband. Whatever they once shared was over, done with, had come to a screeching end.

If only the memories weren't so strong...

She glanced out the window and saw him piling wood on the back porch. Never in her wildest dreams would she have thought her day would end up this way, with her and Dane being stranded together at the cabin—a place they always considered as their favorite getaway spot. During the first two years of their marriage, they would come here every chance they got, but in the past year she could recall them coming only once. Somewhere along the way she had stopped allowing them time even for this.

She sighed deeply, recalling how important it had been to her at the beginning of their marriage for them to make time to talk about matters of interest, whether trivial or important. They had always been attuned to each other, and Dane had always been a good listener, which to her conveyed a sign of caring and respect. But the last couple of times they had tried to talk ended up with them snapping at each other, which only built bitterness and resentment.

The lights blinked and she knew they were about to go out. She was glad that she had taken the initiative to go into the kitchen and scramble up some eggs earlier. And she was inwardly grateful that if she had to get stranded in the cabin during a snowstorm that Dane was here with her. Heaven knows she would have been a basket case had she found herself up here alone.

The lights blinked again before finally going out, but the candles provided the cabin with plenty of light. Not sure if the temperatures outside would cause the pipes to freeze, she had run plenty of water in the bathtub and kitchen sink, and filled every empty jug with water for them to drink. She'd also found batteries to put in the radio so they could keep up with any reports on the weather.

"I saw the lights go out. Are you okay?"

Sienna turned around. Dane was leaning in the doorway with his hands stuck in the pockets of his jeans. The pose made him look incredibly sexy. "Yes, I'm okay. I was able to get the candles all lit and there are plenty more."

"That's good."

"Just in case the pipes freeze and we can't use the shower, I filled the bathtub up with water so we can take a bath that way." At his raised brow she quickly added, "Separately, of course. And I made sure I filled plenty of bottles of drinking water, too."

He nodded. "Sounds like you've been busy."

"So have you. I saw through the window when you put all that wood on the porch. It will probably come in handy."

He moved away from the door. "Yes, and with the electricity out I need to go ahead and get the fire started."

Sienna swallowed as she watched him walk toward her on his way to the fireplace, and not for the first time she thought about how remarkably handsome he was. He had that certain charisma that made women get hot all over just looking at him.

It suddenly occurred to her that he'd already got a fire started, and the way it was spreading through her was about to make her burst into flames.

Chapter 9

"You okay?" Dane asked Sienna as he walked toward her with a smile.

She nodded and cleared her throat. "Yes, why do you ask?"

"Because you're looking at me funny."

"Oh." She was vaguely aware of him walking past her to kneel in front of the fireplace. She turned and watched him, saw him move the wood around before taking a match and lighting it to start a fire. He was so good at kindling things, whether wood or the human body.

"If you like, I can make something for dinner," she decided to say, otherwise she would continue to stand there and say nothing while staring at him. It was hard trying to be normal in a rather awkward situation.

"What are our options?" he asked without looking around.

She chuckled. "An egg sandwich and tea. I made both earlier before the power went off."

He turned at that and his gaze caught hers. A smile crinkled his eyes. "Do I have a choice?"

"Not if you want to eat."

"What about those Girl Scout cookies I found in your car?"

Her eyes narrowed. "They're off-limits. You can have one of the candy bars, but the cookies are mine."

His mouth broke into a wide grin. "You have enough cookies to share, so stop being selfish."

He turned back around and she made a face at him behind his back. He was back to stoking the fire and her gaze went to his hands. Those hands used to be the givers of so much pleasure and almost ran neck and neck with his mouth…but not quite. His mouth was in a class by itself. But still, she could recall those same hands, gentle, provoking, moving all over her body; touching her everywhere and doing things to her that mere hands weren't suppose to do. However, she never had any complaints.

"Did you have any plans for tonight, Sienna?"

His words intruded into her heated thoughts. "No, why?"

"Just wondering. You thought I had a date tonight. What about you?"

She shrugged. "No. As far as I'm concerned, until we sign those final papers, I'm still legally married and wouldn't feel right going out with someone."

He turned around and locked his eyes with hers. "I know what you mean," he said. "I wouldn't feel right going out with someone else."

Heat seeped through her every pore with his words. "So you haven't been dating, either?"

"No."

There were a number of questions she wanted to ask him—how he spent his days, his nights, what his family thought of their pending divorce, what he thought of it, was he ready for it to be over for them to go their separate ways—but there was no way she could ask him any of those things. "I guess I'll go put dinner on the table."

He chuckled. "An egg sandwich and tea?"

"Yes." She turned to leave.

"Sienna?"

She turned back around. "Yes?"

"I don't like being stranded, but since I am, I'm glad it's with you."

For a moment she couldn't say anything, then she cleared her throat while backing up a couple of steps. "Ah, yeah right, same here." She backed up some more then said, "I'll go set out the food now." And then she turned and quickly left the room.

Chapter 10

Sienna glanced up when she heard Dane walk into the kitchen and smiled. "Your feast awaits you."

"Whoopee."

She laughed. "Hey, I know the feeling. I'm glad I had a nice lunch today in celebration. I took on a new client."

Dane came and joined her at the table. "Congratulations."

"Thank you."

She took a bite of her scrambled egg sandwich and a sip of her tea and then said, "It's been a long time since you seemed genuinely pleased with my accomplishments."

He glanced up after taking a sip of his own tea and stared at her for a moment. "I know and I'm sorry about that. It was hard being replaced by your work, Sienna."

She lifted her head and stared at him, met his gaze. She saw the tightness of his jaw and the firm set of his mouth. He actually believed that something could replace him with her and knowing that hit a raw and sensitive nerve. "My work never replaced you, Dane. Why did you begin feeling that way?"

Dane leaned back in his chair, tilted his head slightly. He was more than mildly surprised with her question. It was then he realized that she really didn't know. Hadn't a clue. This was the opportunity that he wanted; what he was hoping they would have. Now was the time to put aside anger, bitterness, foolish pride and whatever else was working at destroying their marriage. Now was the time for complete honesty. "You started missing dinner. Not once but twice, sometimes three times a week. Eventually, you stopped making excuses and didn't show up."

What he'd said was the truth. "But I was working and taking on new clients," she defended. "You said you would understand."

"And I did for a while and up to a point. But there is such a thing as common courtesy and mutual respect, Sienna. In the end I felt like I'd been thrown by the wayside, that you didn't care anymore about us, our love or our marriage."

She narrowed her eyes. "And why didn't you say something?"

"When? I was usually asleep when you got home and when I got up in the morning you were too sleepy to discuss anything. I invited you to lunch several times, but you couldn't fit me into your schedule."

"I had appointments."

"Yes, and I always felt because of it that your clients were more important."

"Still, I wished you would have let me know how you felt," she said, after taking another sip of tea.

"I did, several times. But you weren't listening."

She sighed deeply. "We used to know how to communicate."

"Yes, at one time we did, didn't we?" Dane said quietly. "But I'm also to blame for the failure of our marriage, our lack of communication. And then there were the problems you were having with my parents. When it came to you, I never hesitated letting my parents know when they were out of line and that I wouldn't put up with their treatment of you. But then I felt that at some point you needed to start believing that what they thought didn't matter and stand up to them.

"I honestly thought I was doing the right thing when I decided to just stay out of it and give you the chance to deal with them, to finally put them in their place. Instead, you let them erode away at your security and confidence to the point where you felt you had to prove you were worthy of them…and of me. That's what drove you to be so successful, wasn't it, Sienna? Feeling the need to prove something is what working all those long hours was all about, wasn't it?"

Chapter 11

Sienna quickly got up from the table and walked to the window. It was turning dark but she could clearly see that things hadn't let up. It was still snowing outside, worse than an hour before. She tried to concentrate on what was beyond that window and not on the question Dane had asked her.

"Sienna?"

Moments later she turned back around to face Dane, knowing he was waiting on her response. "What do you want me to say, Dane? Trust me, you don't want to get me started since you've always known how your family felt about me."

His brow furrowed sharply as he moved from the table to join her at the window, coming to stand directly in front of her. "And you've known it didn't matter one damn iota. Why would you let it continue to matter to you?"

She shook her head, tempted to bare her soul but fighting not to. "But you don't understand how important it was for your family to accept me, to love me."

Dane stepped closer, looked into eyes that were fighting to keep tears at bay.

"Wasn't my love enough, Sienna? I'd told you countless time that you didn't marry my family, you married me. I'm not proud of the fact that my parents think too highly of themselves and our family name at times, but I've constantly told you it didn't matter. Why can't you believe me?"

When she didn't say anything, he sighed deeply. "You've been around people with money before. Do all of them act like my parents?"

She thought of her best friend's family. The Steeles. "No."

"Then what should that tell you? They're my parents. I know that they aren't close to being perfect, but I love them."

"And I never wanted to do anything to make you stop loving them."

He reached up and touched her chin. "And that's what this is about, isn't it? Why you filed for a divorce. You thought that you could."

Sienna angrily wiped at a tear she couldn't contain any longer. "I didn't ever want you to have to choose."

Dane's heart ached. Evidently she didn't know just how much he loved her. "There wouldn't have been a choice to make. You're my wife. I love you. I will always love you. When we married, we became one."

He leaned down and brushed a kiss on her cheek, then several. He wanted to devour her mouth, deepen the kiss and escalate it to a level he needed it to be, but he couldn't. He wouldn't. What they needed was to talk, to communicate to try and fix whatever was wrong with their marriage. He pulled back. It was hard when he heard her soft sigh, her heated moan.

He gave in briefly to temptation and tipped her chin up, and placed a kiss on her lips. "There's plenty of hot water still left in the tank," he said softly, stroking her chin. "Go ahead and take a shower before it gets completely dark, and then I'll take one."

He continued to stroke her chin when he added, "Then what I want is for us to do something we should have done months ago, Sienna. I want us to sit down and talk. And I mean to really talk. Regain that level of communication we once had. And what I need to know more than anything is whether my love will ever be just enough for you."

Chapter 12

You're my wife. I love you. I will always love you. When we married, we became one.

Dane's words flowed through Sienna's mind as she stepped into the shower, causing a warm, fuzzy, glowing feeling to seep through her pores. Hope flared within her although she didn't want it to. She hadn't wanted to end her marriage, but when things had begun to get worse between her and Dane, she'd finally decided to take her in-laws' suggestion and get out of their son's life.

Even after three years of seeing how happy she and Dane were together, they still couldn't look beyond her past. They saw her as a nobody, a person who had married their son for his money. She had offered to sign a prenuptial before the wedding and Dane had scoffed at the suggestion, refusing to even draw one up. But still, his parents had made it known each time they saw her just how much they resented the marriage.

And no matter how many times Dane had stood up to them and had put them in their place regarding her, it would only be a matter of time before they resorted to their old ways again, though never in the presence of their son. Maybe Dane was right, and all she'd had to do was tell his parents off once and for all and that would be the end of it, but she never could find the courage to do it.

And what was so hilarious with the entire situation was that she had basically become a workaholic to become successful in her own right so they could see her as their son's equal in every way; and in trying to impress them she had alienated Dane to the point that eventually he would have gotten fed up and asked her for a divorce if she hadn't done so first.

After spending time under the spray of water, she stepped out of the shower, intent on making sure there was enough hot water left for Dane. She tried to put out of her mind the last time she had taken a shower in this stall, and how Dane had joined her in it.

Toweling off, she was grateful she still had some of her belongings at the cabin to sleep in. The last thing she needed was to parade around Dane half naked. Then they would never get any talking done.

She slipped into a T-shirt and a pair of sweatpants she found in one of the drawers. Dane wanted to talk. How could they have honest communication without getting into a discussion about his parents again? She crossed her arms, trying to ignore the chill she was beginning to feel in the air. In order to stay warm they would probably both have to sleep in front of the fireplace tonight. She didn't want to think about what the possibility of doing something like that meant.

While her cell phone still had life, she decided to let her best friend, Vanessa Steele, know that she wouldn't be returning to Charlotte tonight. Dane was right. Not everyone with money acted like his parents. The Steeles, owners of a huge manufacturing company in Charlotte, were just as wealthy as the Bradfords. But they were as down-to-earth as people could get, which proved that not everyone with a lot of money were snobs.

"Hello?"

"Van, it's Sienna."

"Sienna, I was just thinking about you. Did you make it back before that snowstorm hit?"

"No, I'm in the mountains, stranded."

"What! Do you want me to send my cousins to rescue you?"

Sienna smiled. Vanessa was talking about her four single male cousins, Chance, Sebastian, Morgan and Donovan Steele. Sienna had to admit that besides being handsome as sin, they were dependable to a fault. And of all people, she, Vanessa and Vanessa's two younger sisters, Taylor and Cheyenne, should know more than anyone since they had been notorious for getting into trouble while growing up and the brothers four had always been there to bail them out.

"No, I don't need your cousins to come and rescue me."

"What about Dane? You know how I feel about you

divorcing him, Sienna. He's still legally your husband and I think I should let him know where you are and let him decide if he should—"

"Vanessa," Sienna interrupted. "You don't have to let Dane know anything. He's here, stranded with me."

Chapter 13

"How was your shower?" Dane asked Sienna when she returned to the living room a short while later.

"Great. Now it's your turn to indulge."

"Okay." Dane tried not to notice how the candlelight was flickering over Sienna's features, giving them an ethereal glow. He shoved his hands into the pockets of his jeans and for a long moment he stood there staring at her.

She lifted a brow. "What's wrong?"

"I was just thinking how incredibly beautiful you are."

Sienna breathed in deeply, trying to ignore the rush of sensations she felt from his words. "Thank you." Dane had always been a man who'd been free with his compliments. Being apart from him made her realize that was one of the things she missed, among many others.

"I'll be back in a little while," he said before leaving the room.

When he was gone, Sienna remembered the conversation she'd had with Vanessa earlier. Her best friend saw her and Dane being stranded together on the mountain as a twist of fate that Sienna should use to her advantage. Vanessa further thought that for once, Sienna should stand up to the elder Bradfords and not struggle to prove herself to them. Dane had accepted her as she was and now it was time for her to be satisfied and happy with that; after all, she wasn't married to his parents.

A part of Sienna knew that Vanessa was right, but she had been seeking love from others for so long that she hadn't been able to accept that Dane's love was all the love she needed. Before her shower he had asked if his love was enough and now she knew that it was. It was past time for her to acknowledge that fact and to let him know it.

Dane stepped out the shower and began toweling off. The bathroom carried Sienna's scent and the honeysuckle fragrance of the shower gel she enjoyed using.

Given their situation, he really should be worried what they would be faced with if the weather didn't let up in a couple of days with the little bit of food they had. But for now the thought of being stranded here with Sienna overrode all his concerns about that. In his heart, he truly believed they would manage to get through any given situation. Now he had the task of convincing her of that.

He glanced down at his left hand and studied his wedding band. Two weeks ago when he had come here for his pity party, he had taken it off in anger and thrown it in a drawer. It was only when he had returned to Charlotte that he realized he'd left it here in the cabin. At first he had shrugged it off as having no significant meaning since he would be a divorced man in a month's time anyway, but every day he'd felt that a part of him was missing.

In addition to reminding him of Sienna's absence from his life, to Dane, his ring signified their love and the vows that they had made, and a part of him refused to give that up. That's what had driven him back here this weekend—to reclaim the one element of his marriage that he refused to part with yet. Something he felt was rightfully his.

It seemed his ring wasn't the only thing that was rightfully his that he would get the chance to reclaim. More than anything, he wanted his wife back.

Chapter 14

Dane walked into the living room and stopped in his tracks. Sienna sat in front of the fireplace, cross-legged, with a tray of cookies and two glasses of wine. He knew where the cookies had come from, but where the heck had she gotten the wine?

She must have heard him because she glanced over his way and smiled. At that moment he thought she was even more breathtaking than a rose in winter. She licked her lips and immediately he thought she was even more tempting than any decadent dessert.

He cleared his throat. "Where did the wine come from?"

She licked her lips again and his body responded in an unquestionable way. He hoped the candlelight was hiding the physical effect she was having on him. "I found it in one of the kitchen cabinets. I think it's the bottle that was left when we came here to celebrate our first anniversary."

His thoughts immediately remembered that weekend. She had packed a selection of sexy lingerie and he had enjoyed removing each and every piece. She had also given him, among other things, a beautiful gold watch with the inscription engraved, *The Great Dane*. He, in turn, had given her a lover's bracelet, which was similar to a diamond tennis bracelet except that each letter of her name was etched in six of the stones.

He could still remember the single tear that had fallen from her eye when he had placed it on her wrist. That had been a special time for them, memories he would always cherish. That knowledge tightened the love that surrounded his heart. More than anything, he was determined that they settle things this weekend. He needed to make her see that he was hers and she was his. For always.

His lips creased into a smile. "I see you've decided to share the cookies, after all," he said, crossing the room to her.

She chuckled as he dropped down on the floor beside her. "Either that or run the risk of you getting up during the night and eating them all." The firelight danced through the twists on her head, highlighting the medium brown coiled strands with golden flecks. He absolutely loved the natural looking hairstyle on her.

He lifted a dark brow. "Eating them all? Three boxes?"

Her smile grew soft. "Hey, you've been known to overindulge a few times."

He paused as heated memories consumed him, reminding him of those times he had overindulged, especially when it came to making love to her. He recalled one weekend they had gone at it almost nonstop. If she hadn't been on the pill there was no doubt in his mind that that single weekend would have made him a daddy. A very proud one, at that.

She handed him a glass of wine. "May I propose a toast?"

His smile widened. "To what?"

"The return of the Beast from the East."

He switched his gaze from her to glance out the window. Even in the dark he could see the white flecks coming down in droves. He looked back at her and cocked a brow. "We have a reason to celebrate this bad weather?"

She stared at him for a long moment, then said quietly, "Yes. The Beast is the reason we're stranded here together, and even with our low rations of food, I can't think of any other place I'd rather be…than here alone with you."

Chapter 15

Dane stared at Sienna and the intensity of that gaze made her entire body tingle, her nerve endings steam. It was pretty much like the day they'd met, when he'd walked into his father's study. She had looked up, their gazes had connected and the seriousness in the dark irises that had locked with hers had changed her life forever. She had fallen in love with him then and there.

Dane didn't say anything for a long moment as he continued to look at her, and then he lifted his wine-glass and said huskily, "To the Beast…who brought me Beauty."

His words were like a sensuous stroke down her spine, and the void feeling she'd had during the past few months was slowly fading away. After the toast was made and they had both taken sips of their wine,

Dane placed his glass aside and then relieved her of hers. He then slowly leaned forward and captured her mouth, tasting the wine, relishing her delectable flavor. How had she gone without this for six months? How had she survived? she wondered as his tongue devoured hers, battering deep in the heat of her mouth, licking and sucking as he wove his tongue in and out between teeth, gum and whatever wanted to serve as a barrier.

He suddenly pulled back and stared at her. A smile touched the corners of his lips. "I could keep going and going, but before we go any further we need to talk, determine what brought us to this point so it won't ever be allowed to happen again. I don't want us to ever let anything or anyone have power, more control over the vows we made three years ago."

Sienna nodded, thinking the way the firelight was dancing over his dark skin was sending an erotic frisson up her spine. "All right."

He stood. "I'll be right back."

Sienna lifted a brow, wondering where he was going and watched as he crossed the room to open the desk drawer. Like her, he had changed into a T-shirt and a pair of sweats, and as she watched him she found it difficult to breathe. He moved in such a manly way, each movement a display of fine muscles and limbs and how they worked together in graceful coordination, perfect precision. Watching him only knocked her hormones out of whack.

He returned moments later with pens and paper in hand. There was a serious expression on his face when he handed her a sheet of paper and a pen and kept the same for himself. "I want us to write down all the things we feel went wrong with our marriage, being honest to include everything. And then we'll discuss them."

She looked down at the pen and paper and then back at him. "You want me to write them down?"

"Yes, and I'll do the same."

Sienna nodded and watched as he began writing on his paper, wondering what he was jotting down. She leaned back and sighed, wondering if she could air their dirty laundry on paper, but it seemed he had no such qualms. Most couples sought the helpful guidance of marriage counselors when they found themselves in similar situations, but she hadn't given them that chance. But at this point, she would do anything to save her marriage.

So she began writing, being honest with herself and with him.

Chapter 16

Dane finished writing and glanced over at Sienna. She was still at it and had a serious expression on her features. He studied the contours of her face and his gaze dropped to her neck, and he noticed the thin gold chain. She was still wearing the heart pendant he'd given her as a wedding gift.

Deep down, Dane believed this little assignment was what they needed as the first step in repairing what had gone wrong in their marriage. Having things written down would make it easier to stay focused and not go off on a tangent. And it made one less likely to give in to the power of the mind, the wills and emotions. He wanted them to concentrate on those destructive elements and forces that had eroded away at what should have been a strong relationship.

She glanced up and met his gaze as she put the pen aside. She gave him a wry smile. "Okay, that's it."

He reached out and took her hand in his, tightening his hold on it when he saw a look of uncertainty on her face. "All right, what do you have?"

She gave him a sheepish grimace. "How about you going first?"

He gently squeezed her hand. "How about if we go together? I'll start off and then we'll alternate."

She nodded. "What if we have the same ones?"

"That will be okay. We'll talk about all of them." He picked up his piece of paper.

"First on my list is communication."

Sienna smiled ruefully. "It's first on mine, too. And I agree that we need to talk more, without arguing, not that you argued. I think you would hold stuff in when I made you upset instead of getting it out and speaking your mind."

Dane stared at her for a moment, then a smile touched his lips. "You're right, you know. I always had to plug in the last word and I did it because I knew it would piss you off."

"Well, stop doing it."

He grinned. "Okay. The next time I'll hang around for us to talk through things. But then you're going to have to make sure that you're available when we need to talk. You can't let anything, not even your job, get in the way of us communicating."

"Okay, I agree."

"Now, what's next on your list?" he asked.

She looked up at him and smiled. "Patience. I know

you said that I don't have patience, but neither do you. But you used to."

Dane shook his head. "Yeah, I lost my patience when you did. I thought to myself, why should I be patient with you when you weren't doing the same with me? Sometimes I think you thought I enjoyed knowing you had a bad day or didn't make a sale, and that wasn't it at all. At some point what was suddenly important to you wasn't important to me anymore."

"And because of it, we both became detached," Sienna said softly.

"Yes, we did." He reached out and lifted her chin. "I promise to do a better job of being patient, Sienna."

"So will I, Dane."

They alternated, going down the list. They had a number of the same things on both lists and they discussed everything in detail, acknowledging their faults and what they could have done to make things better. They also discussed what they would do in the future to strengthen their marriage.

"That's all I have on my list," Dane said a while later. "Do you have anything else?"

Sienna's finger glided over her list. For a short while she thought about pretending she didn't have anything else, but they had agreed to be completely honest. They had definitely done so when they had discussed her spending more time at work than at home.

"So what's the last thing on your list, Sienna? What do you see as one of the things that went wrong with our marriage?"

She lifted her chin and met his gaze and said, "My inability to stand up to your parents."

He looked at her with deep, dark eyes. "Okay, then. Let's talk about that."

Chapter 17

Dane waited patiently for Sienna to begin talking and gently rubbed the backside of her hand while doing so. He'd known the issue of his parents had always been a challenge to her. Over the years, he had tried to make her see that how the elder Bradfords felt didn't matter. What he failed to realize, accept and understand was that it *did* matter…to her.

She had grown up in a family without love for so long that when they married, she not only sought his love, but that of his family. Being accepted meant a lot to her, and her expectations of the Bradfords, given how they operated and their family history, were too high.

They weren't a close-knit bunch, never had been and never would be. His parents had allowed their own parents to decide their future, including who they married.

When they had come of age, arranged marriages were the norm within the Bradfords' circle. His father had once confided to him one night after indulging in too many drinks that his mother had not been his choice for a wife. That hadn't surprised Dane, nor had it bothered him, since he would bet that his father probably hadn't been his mother's choice of a husband, either.

"I don't want to rehash the past, Dane," Sienna finally said softly, looking at the blaze in the fireplace instead of at him. "But something you said earlier tonight has made me think about a lot of things. You love your parents, but you've never hesitated in letting them know when you felt they were wrong, nor have you put up with their crap when it came to me."

She switched her gaze from the fire to him. "The problem is that *I* put up with their crap when it came to me. And you were right. I thought I had to actually prove something to them, show them I was worthy of you and your love. And I've spent the better part of a year and a half doing that and all it did was bring me closer and closer to losing you. I'm sure they've been walking around with big smiles on their faces since you got the divorce petition. But I refuse to let them be happy at my expense and my own heartbreak."

She scooted closer to Dane and splayed her hands against his chest. "It's time I became more assertive with your parents, Dane. Because it's not about them—it's about us. I refuse to let them make me feel unworthy any longer, because I am worthy to be loved by you. I don't have anything to prove. They either accept me as I am or not at all. The only person who matters anymore is you."

With his gaze holding hers, Dane lifted one of her hands off his chest and brought it to his lips, and placed a kiss on the palm. "I'm glad you've finally come to realize that, Sienna. And I wholeheartedly understand and agree. I was made to love you, and if my parents never accept that then it's their loss, not ours."

Tears constricted Sienna's throat and she swallowed deeply before she could find her voice to say, "I love you, Dane. I don't want the divorce. I never did. I want to belong to you and I want you to belong to me. I just want to make you happy."

"And I love you, too, Sienna, and I don't want the divorce, either. My life will be nothing without you being a part of it. I love you so much and I've missed you."

And with his heart pounding hard in his chest, he leaned over and captured her lips, intent on showing her just what he meant.

Chapter 18

This is homecoming, Sienna thought as she was quickly consumed by the hungry onslaught of Dane's kiss. All the hurt and anger she'd felt for six months was being replaced by passion of the most heated kind. All she could think about was the desire she was feeling being back in the arms of the man she loved and who loved her.

This was the type of communication she'd always loved, where she could share her thoughts, feelings and desires with Dane without uttering a single word. It was where their deepest emotions and what was in their inner hearts spoke for them, expressing things so eloquently and not leaving any room for misunderstandings.

He pulled back slightly, his lips hovering within inches of hers. He reached out and caressed her cheek, and as if she needed his taste again, her lips automatically parted. A slow, sensual acknowledgement of understanding tilted the corners of his mouth into a smile. Then he leaned closer and kissed her again, longer and harder, and the only thing she could do was to wrap her arms around him and silently thank God for reuniting her with this very special man.

Dane was hungry for the taste of his wife and at that moment, as his heart continued to pound relentlessly in his chest, he knew he had to make love to her, to show her in every way what she meant to him, had always meant to him and would always mean to him.

He pulled back slightly and the moisture that was left on her lips made his stomach clench. He leaned forward and licked them dry, or tried to, but her scent was driving him to do more. "Please let me make love to you, Sienna," he whispered, leaning down and resting his forehead against hers.

She leaned back and cupped his chin with her hand. "Oh, yes. I want you to make love to me, Dane. I've missed being with you so much I ache."

"Oh, baby, I love you." He pulled her closer, murmured the words in her twisted locks, kissed her cheek, her temple, her lips, and he cupped her buttocks, practically lifting her off the floor in the process. His breath came out harsh, ragged, as the chemistry between them sizzled. There was only one way to drench their fire.

He stretched out with her in front of the fireplace as he began removing her clothes and then his. Moments later, the blaze from the fire was a flickering light across their naked skin. And then he began kissing her all over, leaving no part of her untouched, determined to quench his hunger and his desire. He had missed the taste of her and was determined to be reacquainted in every way he could think of.

"Dane…"

Her tortured moan ignited the passion within him and he leaned forward to position his body over hers, letting his throbbing erection come to rest between her thighs, gently touching the entrance of her moist heat. He lifted his head to look down at her, wanting to see her expression the exact moment their bodies joined again.

Chapter 19

Sienna stared into Dane's eyes, the heat and passion she saw in them making her shiver. The love she recognized made her heart pound, and the desire she felt for him sent surges and surges of sensations through every part of her body, especially the area between her legs, making her thighs quiver.

"You're my everything, Sienna," he whispered as he began easing inside of her. His gaze was locked with hers as his voice came out in a husky tone. "I need you like I need air to breathe, water for thirst and food for nourishment. Oh, baby, my life has been so empty since you've been gone. I love and need you."

His words touched her and when he was embedded inside of her to the hilt, she arched her back, needing and wanting even more of him. She gripped his shoulders with her fingers as liquid fire seemed to flow to all parts of her body.

And at that moment she forgot everything—the Beast from the East, their limited supply of food and the fact they were stranded together in a cabin with barely enough heat. The only thing that registered in her mind was that they were together and expressing their love in a way that literally touched her soul.

He continued to stroke her, in and out, and with each powerful thrust into her body she moaned out his name and told him of her love. She was like a bow whose strings were being stretched to the limit each and every time he drove into her, and she met his thrusts with her own eager ones.

And then she felt it, the strength like a volcano erupting as he continued to stroke her to oblivion. Her body splintered into a thousand pieces as an orgasm ripped through her, almost snatching her breath away. And when she felt him buck, tighten his hold on her hips and thrust into her deeper, she knew that same powerful sensation had taken hold of him, as well.

"Sienna!"

He screamed her name and growled a couple of words that were incoherent to her ears. She tightened her arms around his neck, needing to be as close to him as she could get. She knew in her heart at that moment that things were going to be fine. She and Dane had proved that when it came to the power of love, it was never too late.

Sienna awoke the following morning naked, in front of the fireplace and cuddled in her husband's arms with a blanket covering them. After yawning, she raised her chin and glanced over at him and met his gaze head-on. The intensity in the dark eyes staring back at her shot heat through all parts of her body. She couldn't help but recall last night and how they had tried making up for all the time they had been apart.

"It's gone," Dane said softly, pulling her closer into his arms.

She lifted a brow. "What's gone?"

"The Beast."

She tilted her head to glance out the window and he was right. Although snow was still falling, it wasn't the violent blizzard that had been unleashed the day before. It was as if the weather had served the purpose it had come for and had made its exit. She smiled. Evidently, someone up there knew she and Dane's relationship was meant to be saved and had stepped in to salvage it.

She was about to say something when suddenly there was a loud pounding at the door. She and Dane looked at each other, wondering who would be paying them a visit to the cabin at this hour and in this weather.

Chapter 20

Sienna, like Dane, had quickly gotten dressed and was now staring at the four men who were standing in the doorway…those handsome Steele brothers. She smiled, shaking her head. Vanessa had evidently called her cousins to come rescue her, anyway.

"Vanessa called us," Chance Steele, the oldest of the pack, said by way of explanation. "It just so happened that we were only a couple of miles down the road at our own cabin." A smile touched his lips. "She was concerned that the two of you were here starving to death and asked us to share some of our rations."

"Thanks, guys," Dane said, gladly accepting the box Sebastian Steele was handing him. "Come on in. And although we've had plenty of heat to keep us warm, I have to admit our food supply was kind of low."

As soon as the four entered, all eyes went to Sienna. Although the brothers knew Dane because their families sometimes ran in the same social circles, as well as the fact that Dane and Donovan Steele had graduated from high school the same year, she knew their main concern was for her. She had been their cousin Vanessa's best friend for years, and as a result they had sort of adopted her as their little cousin, as well.

"You okay?" Morgan Steele asked her, although Sienna knew she had to look fine; probably like a woman who'd been made love to all night, and she wasn't ashamed of that fact. After all, Dane *was* her husband. But the Steeles knew about her pending divorce, so she decided to end their worries.

She smiled and moved closer to Dane. He automatically wrapped his arms around her shoulders and brought her closer to his side. "Yes, I'm wonderful," she said, breaking the subtle tension she felt in the room. "Dane and I have decided we don't want a divorce and intend to stay together and make our marriage work."

The relieved smiles on the faces of the four men were priceless. "That's wonderful. We're happy for you," Donovan Steele said, grinning.

"We apologize if we interrupted anything, but you know Vanessa," Chance said, smiling. "She wouldn't let up. We would have come sooner but the bad weather kept us away."

"Your timing was perfect," Dane said, grinning. "We appreciate you even coming out now. I'm sure the roads weren't their best."

"No, but my new truck managed just fine," Sebastian

said proudly. "Besides, we're going fishing later. We would invite you to join us, Dane, but I'm sure you can think of other ways you'd prefer to spend your time."

Dane smiled as he glanced down and met Sienna's gaze. "Oh, yeah, I can definitely think of a few."

The power had been restored and a couple of hours later, after eating a hefty breakfast of pancakes, sausage, grits and eggs, and drinking what Dane had to admit was the best coffee he'd had in a long time, Dane and Sienna were wrapped in each other's arms in the king-size bed. Sensations flowed through her just thinking about how they had ached and hungered for each other, and the fierceness of their lovemaking to fulfill that need and greed.

"Now will you tell me what brought you to the cabin?" Sienna asked, turning in Dane's arms and meeting his gaze.

"My wedding band." He then told her why he'd come to the cabin two weeks ago and how he'd left the ring behind. "It was as if without that ring on my finger, my connection to you was gone. I had to have it back so I came here for it."

Sienna nodded, understanding completely. That was one of the reasons she hadn't removed hers. Reaching out she cupped his stubble jaw in her hand and then leaned over and kissed him softly. "Together forever, Mr. Bradford."

Dane smiled. "Yes, Mrs. Bradford, together forever. We've proved that when it comes to true love, it's never too late."

* * * * *

NEVER TOO LATE is part of
Brenda Jackson's
FORGED OF STEELE *series.*
Don't miss the latest story,
POSSESSED BY PASSION
Available March 2016 from Kimani Romance.

And be sure to pick up the other stories in
FORGED OF STEELE*:*

SOLID SOUL
NIGHT HEAT
BEYOND TEMPTATION
RISKY PLEASURES
IRRESISTIBLE FORCES
INTIMATE SEDUCTION
HIDDEN PLEASURES
A STEELE FOR CHRISTMAS
PRIVATE ARRANGEMENTS

Available from Kimani Romance

COMING NEXT MONTH FROM

Available March 1, 2016

#2431 THE CEO'S UNEXPECTED CHILD

Billionaires and Babies • by Andrea Laurence

When a fertility clinic makes a mistake, a recent widow discovers her infant daughter doesn't belong to her late husband, but to a billionaire set on claiming his new family...by any means.

#2432 THE SEAL'S SECRET HEIRS

Texas Cattleman's Club: Lies and Lullabies
by Kat Cantrell

A former Navy SEAL comes home to his greatest challenge yet—surprise fatherhood of secret twins—only to discover his high school sweetheart is his children's social worker. Will the first-time father get a second shot at real love?

#2433 SNOWBOUND WITH THE BOSS

Pregnant by the Boss • by Maureen Child

When gaming tycoon Sean Ryan is stranded with irascible, irresistible contractor Kate Wells, the temptation to keep each other warm proves overwhelming. Dealing with unexpected feelings is hard enough, but what about an unexpected pregnancy? They're about to find out...

#2434 ONE SECRET NIGHT, ONE SECRET BABY

Moonlight Beach Bachelors • by Charlene Sands

Though Hollywood heartthrob Dylan McKay has no memory of that fateful night with his sister's best friend, he must face the music. He's made her pregnant and will make her his bride. But soon the shocking, unforgettable truth emerges...

#2435 THE RANCHER'S MARRIAGE PACT

Texas Extreme • by Kristi Gold

Marrying his sexy interior designer is convenient enough for rich rancher Dallas Calloway. He'll get his inheritance and she'll get a new lease on life. Then the business arrangement turns into more than they bargain for...

#2436 HIS SECRETARY'S SURPRISE FIANCÉ

Bayou Billionaires • by Joanne Rock

Winning at any cost might work on the football field, but will demanding a fake engagement really keep billionaire sportsman Dempsey Reynaud's alluring assistant in his life?

When a fertility clinic makes a mistake, a recent widow discovers her infant daughter doesn't belong to her late husband, but to a billionaire set on claiming his new family...by any means.

Read on for a sneak peek at THE CEO'S UNEXPECTED CHILD, the latest in the bestselling ***BILLIONAIRES AND BABIES*** *miniseries*

Claire looked completely panicked by the thought of Luca having access to her child.

Their child.

It seemed so wrong for him to have a child with a woman he'd never met. But now that he had a living, breathing daughter, he wasn't about to sit back and pretend it didn't happen. Eva was probably the only child he would ever have, and he'd already missed months of her life. That would not continue.

"We can and we will." Luca spoke up at last. "Eva is my daughter, and I've got the paternity test results to prove it. There's not a judge in the county of New York who won't grant me emergency visitation while we await our court date. They will say when and where and how often you have to give her to me."

Claire sat, her mouth agape at his words. "She's just a baby. She's only six months old. Why fight me for her just so you can hand her over to a nanny?"

Luca laughed at her presumptuous tone. "What makes you so certain I'll have a nanny for her?"

"You're a rich, powerful, unmarried businessman. You're better suited to run a corporation than to change a diaper. I'm willing to bet you don't have the first clue of how to care for an infant, much less the time."

Luca just shook his head and sat forward in his seat. "You know very little about me, *tesorino*, you've said so yourself, so don't presume anything about me."

Claire narrowed her gaze at him. She definitely didn't like him pushing her. And he was pushing her. Partially because he liked to see the fire in her eyes and the flush of her skin, and partially because it was necessary to get through to her.

Neither of them had asked for this to happen to them, but she needed to learn she wasn't in charge. They had to cooperate if this awkward situation was going to improve. He'd started off nice, politely requesting to see Eva, and he'd been flatly ignored. As each request was met with silence, he'd escalated the pressure. That's how they'd ended up here today. If she pushed him any further, he would start playing hardball. He didn't want to, but he would crush her like his restaurants' competitors.

"We can work together and play nice, or my lawyer here can make things very difficult for you. As he said, it's your choice."

"What are you suggesting, Mr. Moretti?" her lawyer asked.

"I'm suggesting we both take a little time away from our jobs and spend it together."

Looking for more wealthy bachelors? Fear not!
Be sure to collect these sexy reads from
Harlequin® Presents and Harlequin® Blaze!

A FORBIDDEN TEMPTATION
by Anne Mather

Jack Connolly isn't looking for a woman—until he meets Grace Spencer! Trapped in a fake relationship to safeguard her family, Grace knows giving in to Jack would risk *everything* she holds dear… But will she surrender to the forbidden?

Available February 16, 2016

SWEET SEDUCTION
by Daire St. Denis

When Daisy Sinclair finds out the man she spent the night with is her ex-husband's new lawyer, she flips. Is Jamie Forsythe in on helping steal her family bakery? Or was their sweet seduction the real thing?

Available March 1, 2016

www.Harlequin.com

HPB0216